LIFE. REMIXED.

An Interactive Musical Story of a DJ Out of Sync

"Stranger Things meets Breaking Bad in a 1990s underground rave, with immersive Easter eggs at every turn."
- Skylar P.

AARON TRAYLOR

Life. Remixed.

Aaron Traylor

Published by Aaron Traylor, 2024.

LIFE. REMIXED.

First edition. September 9, 2024.

ISBN: 979-8227271754

Written by Aaron Traylor.

Foreword

I've known Aaron for many years now. We have traveled together, danced together, even started a business together. We laughed a million laughs and even cried together.

In all of these years though, I've never heard the stories that are included in this book. While reading it, I often would put the book down and ask "was it real or a dream in Aaron's head?"

If nothing else, I was very much entertained. It's set in the 90s, which was an amazing decade. Hip hop began its meteoric rise and 128 bpm dance music led to underground raves. As a DJ myself and someone almost the same age as Aaron, I got to experience it similar to him (minus many of the extremes he endured). He nails this time period.

His ups and downs as a radio and rave DJ are a rollercoaster ride for sure, but through it all, his obsession with music is what shines here.

Enjoy the read. Enjoy the journey.

Joe Bunn

The DJs Vault

Crate Hackers

Author Notes

While some names, locations, and events have been changed or merged, this story draws from my firsthand observations and experiences within the radio industry and the underground music scene of my generation. I hope that my personal journey will offer insights to those who love music and are in search of life's deeper meaning.

Dedicated to

Anneka

My daughter,

You know, you mean the world to me. I can't imagine what my life would be like without you in it. You've given me a reason to keep going and be my best self. I just want you to know how much you matter to me, and how grateful I am for you every single day.

Dad

Grab Your Headphones:

Push play on the soundtrack.
The songs have meaning.

Scan for Clues:

Throughout the story, hidden activities are dispersed,
Click to engage in interactive experiences.

Prologue:

"Get Busy Child" by The Crystal Method

[125 BPM]

"Look up, Aaron. Look UP!"

The needle touched the vinyl, and the world held its breath.

In an abandoned Spokane warehouse, bodies moved as one. Sweat glistened under strobes, faces locked in ecstasy. At the epicenter of this human chaos stood a figure, hunched over a set of turntables like a man possessed.

This was Aaron aka. the laughing stock of Sacajawea Junior High, now the undisputed king of the Northwest rave scene. His hands flew over the mixer like *magic*.

But tonight was different. Tonight, Aaron was about to unleash something that would change everything.

The vinyl beneath his fingers felt unnaturally cold, as if touched by something from beyond this world. In the crowd, a familiar face caught his eye – Rachel, the girl he'd loved since before he knew what love was. She smiled, oblivious to the storm that was about to break.

The beat dropped, and reality itself seemed to fracture.

The sounds blasting out were totally alien, like nothing we'd ever heard. It was beauty and terror, ecstasy and agony, all wrapped into a rhythm that spoke to the very core of human existence. As the track built, Aaron felt a surge of power coursing through him. He was no longer just mixing music; he was conducting the very frequencies of the universe.

In the crowd, something shifted. The dance became frenzied, almost violent. Eyes rolled back in heads, mouths opened in silent screams. And at the edges of the warehouse, shadows began to move of their own accord.

Aaron's best friend Eddie, his eyes wild and unfocused, stumbled towards the DJ booth. "A-Aaron," he stuttered, his voice barely audible over the thunderous bass. "S-something's wrong. I c-can see... oh God, I can see..."

But Aaron couldn't stop. The music had taken on a life of its own, pulling him deeper into its dark embrace. As the track reached its climax, he looked up and saw... something. A tear in the fabric of reality, in time with the beat.

And through that tear, eyes looked back at him. Ancient, hungry eyes.

In that moment, Aaron understood the true power of what he'd created. This wasn't just music. It was a key, unlocking doors that were never meant to be opened.

As the final notes faded, silence fell over the warehouse. But it wasn't the exhausted, satisfied silence that usually followed a killer set. This was the silence of a tomb, heavy with the gravity of something unchangeable.

Aaron looked out over the crowd, his heart pounding. Some lay motionless on the floor, while others stared blankly into space, tears streaming down their cheeks. Rachel was nowhere to be seen.

In the distance, sirens wailed. But it wasn't the police Aaron feared now. It was what he'd unleashed – a force beyond his comprehension, drawn by the siren song of his creation.

As he stood there, the weight of his actions crashing down upon him, Aaron realized that his journey had only just begun. He had wanted fame, acceptance, love. Instead, he had opened a Pandora's box of sound, unleashing forces that threatened not just his world, but the very fabric of reality itself.

The needle lifted, the record stopped spinning. But the real story – a tale of music and madness, of love and loss, of damnation and redemption – was about to begin.

And somewhere in the shadows, something ancient and terrible stirred, awakened by the frequency of fate.

Chapter 1:

"Loser" by Beck

[85.5 BPM]

Spokane, Washington, 1993. A town where excitement went to die, nestled on Interstate 90 between Seattle's grunge and Salt Lake's... well, salt. Our claim to fame? A nearly two-decade-old World Expo that left us with Riverfront Park – a glorified remnant of past glory that seemed to mock our small-town aspirations.

I'm Aaron, and this is the story of how I became "Dookie." Yes, Dookie. But let's get one thing straight – this isn't some cute playground nickname. It's the kind of word that makes even the toughest lunch lady wince.

The fluorescent lights of Sacajawea Junior High buzzed overhead, casting a sickly glow on the linoleum battlefield of adolescence. As I stood in the locker room, surrounded by jocks who seemed to have more hair gel than brain cells, I reached for my yellow Walkman – my shield against the cruel world of junior high.

I turned up the volume, letting hip-hop music drown out the mocking voices around me. As the beat filled my ears, my head started its familiar nodding - a habit born from years of anxiety. It was an unconscious movement, something my body did even without music, as if always searching for a rhythm to escape into. This constant need to move, to find a beat, was my way of coping with the stress that seemed to follow me everywhere.

But this wasn't just about drowning out noise. As the music filled my ears, I felt something shift. The locker room seemed to fade away, replaced by a pulsing, otherworldly landscape of sound. It was as if the music opened a portal to another frequency, one where the petty cruelties of junior high couldn't touch me.

I should've been at home, faking a stomach ache like I'd done a hundred times before. But no, today I decided to be brave. Today, I was trying out for the wrestling team. Why, you ask? Two words: Rachel Meyers.

Rachel was the kind of girl who made you forget how to breathe. Her hair cascaded down her back like a waterfall of dark chocolate, and when she flipped it over her shoulder, I swear time itself paused to admire the view. She sat in front of me in Algebra, and I spent more time studying the curve of her neck than I did quadratic equations.

But Rachel liked the smart, sporty Caltech type. And I... well, I was more of a Gameboy than a Joe Montana. My idea of athleticism was speed-running Sonic the Hedgehog while demolishing a family-size bag of Cool Ranch Doritos. So, in a moment of what I can only describe as temporary insanity, I decided to try out for wrestling.

That's when Ricky Snyder made his grand entrance. Picture the love child of Zack Morris and a young Jean-Claude Van Damme, but with none of the charm and twice the douchebaggery. He sauntered over, a towel barely clinging to his waist, and yanked my headphones off.

"What's this crap you're listening to, lardass?" Ricky sneered, his teeth unnaturally white against his Fruit-of-the-Loom's.

My head kept nodding, more frantically now, as if trying to hold onto the beat that was no longer there. I panicked, seeking a witty response. Something cool, something that would make me fit in. "Uh, it's... it's the new Pharcyde album. You probably wouldn't understand it, it's pretty underground."

The locker room fell silent. Ricky's face twisted in disbelief. "The Pharcyde? Underground? Are you kidding me?"

I felt my face burning hotter than the inside of a Hot Pocket. "I... I meant..."

"Shut up, fatso," Ricky cut me off. "You wouldn't know good music if it slapped you in your triple chin."

As Ricky and his cronies closed in, I fumbled with my Walkman, desperately trying to escape back into that other frequency. I cranked the volume to max, the bassline of "Passin' Me By" thumping in my ears as I squeezed my eyes shut.

Momentarily, it was functional. The world faded away, replaced by that otherworldly landscape. My fingers tapped out the rhythm on my leg, perfectly in sync with the beat. In this place, I was untouchable. I was...

Suddenly airborne. My eyes snapped open as Ricky and his goon squad hoisted me up, my precious Walkman clattering to the floor. And then it happened. That fateful, awful, no-good moment that would define the rest of my junior high career.

I won't go into the gory details. Let's just say those cafeteria Sloppy Joes made an encore appearance, and in that instant, I went from "weird fat kid" to "Dookie."

As I sat in the post office bathroom across the street, pants around my ankles, waiting for my mom to pick me up, I realized I was thinking about Rachel. She'd been there, in the gym, when it all went down. The only one who didn't laugh. The only one who looked... concerned?

But it didn't matter now. I was the boy who defecated himself during wrestling tryouts. The legend that would be passed down through generations of Sacajawea students.

As I listened to the postman awkwardly try to explain the situation to my mom over the phone, his voice faded to a distant buzz as I fumbled with my yellow Walkman, desperate for distraction. I cranked the volume, scanning frantically through FM and AM stations. Static and fragments of songs blurred together, matching the chaos in my head.

"Come on," I muttered, shaking the device. "There's gotta be something..."

Suddenly, a deep, confident voice cut through the noise:

"Join us tonight as we explore the unexplained, the supernatural..."

For thirty seconds, I was transported. The voice spoke of aliens and conspiracies, captivating and strange. As quickly as it appeared, it faded back to static. But something had shifted. My breathing slowed, my hands steadied.

This humiliating moment would spark a journey from junior high laughingstock to the core of Spokane's underground rave scene. In the coming years, I'd swap my Walkman for turntables, my embarrassing nickname for a DJ moniker, and my desperate need for acceptance for something far riskier. Little did I know, I'd soon be searching for that elusive voice in the darkness once more.

But that's getting ahead of ourselves. For now, I was just a kid with a messy problem and a supernatural connection to music that wouldn't stop playing, even when the world around me fell silent.

Welcome to my world. It's a little messy, but I promise, it's one *hell* of a ride.

Chapter 2:

"Heaven Scent" by Bedrock, John Digweed

[135 BPM]

Saturday nights in Spokane are legendary... for their mind-numbing boredom. At eighteen, with limited entertainment options, I found myself trapped in a cycle of dullness that seemed inescapable. Life in this town ticked away with monotonous precision, each moment an echo of missed opportunities.

I had graduated high school and was now living in my mother's old house, a modest two-bedroom starter on the outskirts of town. It was a condition of my enrollment at the local community college - Mom's way of giving me a taste of freedom while keeping me on a short leash.

Mom had remarried last fall, a whirlwind romance with a cowboy from Montana that left me reeling. Before I knew it, she was packing up her life and moving two states away, leaving me to navigate the treacherous waters of early adulthood in this sleepy town.

As I sat in the living room, my fingers unconsciously tapping out a rhythm on the arm of the couch, I couldn't help but feel resentment and gratitude. The house felt empty without Mom, but the freedom was intoxicating.

"It's time you learn to stand on your own two feet, Aaron," Mom had said, handing me the keys with pride and worry in her eyes. "But remember, this isn't a free ride. You stay in college, keep your grades up, and follow the rules - no parties, no overnight guests, and absolutely no drugs. You do that, and the rent's on me."

It was a sweet deal, I had to admit. My own space, free from the watchful eyes of parents, yet with a safety net firmly in place. Mom had always been good like that - pushing me to grow while making sure I didn't fall too hard. I knew the less I shared about my life, the longer I could keep this arrangement. So, I became an expert at selective storytelling, painting a picture of responsible adulthood that often diverged from reality.

Most weekends followed a predictable pattern. Rachel and Eddie would show up early, we'd order a pizza, and spend hours debating what to do with our evening. By the time we'd reach a decision, it was usually too late to do anything, or we'd talked ourselves into staying in. Again.

Rachel, with her dark hair and quick wit, was the brains of our little group. She'd been the first kid in class to load cheat codes onto her Nintendo back in junior high, and that early love had blossomed into something more. Now, she dived deep into the world of code, searching for vulnerabilities in a local company's network – just for fun, of course.

As I watched her fingers fly over her bulky laptop, I couldn't help but marvel at how she seemed to exist in two worlds at once. Here she was, in my living room, but her mind was navigating virtual landscapes I could barely comprehend. It was fascinating and a little intimidating.

"Aaron, are you gonna help us figure out what we're doing tonight?" **Rachel**'s voice cut through my thoughts as she tossed a half-eaten pizza crust my way. "Or are you just gonna sit there for the next four hours trying to call that radio show? That 'Johnny' loudmouth will probably hang up on you anyway. You know he only talks to chicks."

def access_portal():

 # >> Accessing secure portals...

INCOMING TRANSMISSION

01111001 01101111 01110101 00100000 01101101 01100001
01100100 01100101 00100000 01101101 01100101 00100000 01100110
01100101 01100101 01101100 00100000 01110011 01100001 01100110
01100101

portal_link = https://bit.ly/3T3ndTd
return portal_link
 # System shutdown: End of Line.

Rachel and I had grown closer since the legendary locker room incident at Sacajawea Junior High. I think she pitied me at first - after all, when a guy accidentally soils himself in front of his entire wrestling team, he needs all the support he can get. Both she and Eddie had seen me through that traumatic period, a gesture I'd never forget.

But our dynamic had shifted. Rachel only hung out with us when she was between classes. To her, I was the "cute boy" - emphasis on boy, not boyfriend. She tolerated Eddie, but lately, it felt like we were more his babysitters than his friends. His increasing drug experimentation was putting a damper on our usual fun.

"Yo, dude, check this out," Eddie's voice broke through my thoughts as he tossed a crumpled piece of paper onto my greasy napkin. "Found this in my wallet."

I smoothed out the paper to reveal a crudely typed flyer. The word "RAVE" was highlighted, along with today's date and a voicemail number. As I stared at the flyer, a strange feeling washed over me. It was as if the paper itself was vibrating, calling out to me in a language I didn't yet understand.

"Oh!" Rachel exclaimed, snatching the flyer from my hands. Her eyes lit up with that familiar spark of curiosity. "I've heard about these! They're supposed to be amazing. My coding buddy in Seattle was telling me about the insane light shows they program for these things."

"Rave?" I echoed, my curiosity getting the best of me. "Isn't that like a punk mosh pit or something? I heard they get pretty wild."

"I'm not sure exactly," Rachel admitted. "But apparently, there's a lot of dancing involved. We should check it out!"

As Rachel grabbed her coat and started applying lipstick, I felt apprehension bubbling up inside me. Dancing had never been my forte, but I was always up for something new. It wasn't often that anything different came through our sleepy town.

"Yeah, why not?" Eddie chimed in, reaching for the last slice of pizza. "Beats staring at these four walls. I'm starting to fry anyway."

With a shrug, I dialed the number on the flyer. As the phone rang, I couldn't shake the feeling that something momentous was about to happen. Little did I know, this night would change the course of my life forever.

"Let's do this," I said, hanging up the phone. "Rachel, you're driving. Eddie, you're in the back."

As we piled into Rachel's car, the static of 97.3 "The X" FM faded away, replaced by the hum of the engine and the excitement in the air. Spokane's quiet streets seemed to whisper of the adventure that lay ahead, and for once, I felt the suffocating boredom of our small town begin to lift.

The Masonic Temple loomed before us, a line of eager ravers snaking around the block. The air buzzed with anticipation, the crowd a sea of oversized clothing, Adidas shoes, and hip bags. Some girls sported cartoon-like makeup, their hair clipped back for uninhibited dancing. A few even had baby pacifiers dangling from cords around their necks - a puzzling accessory that I'd later learn was part of the rave culture.

After a thirty-minute wait and forking over the three-dollar admission, we stepped into a world that would forever alter my perception of music, connection, and belonging.

The change hit like a punch. The dark, foggy building throbbed, and it wasn't just the music. Hundreds of misfits like me packed the place. I recognized faces from high school, including some who still knew me as my nickname. But here, those labels seemed to melt away.

For once, I belonged. Not with the jocks or popular kids, but with the weirdos and nerds who never fit in. Here, we all moved to the same beat.

I watched a guy with thick glasses and a Star Trek t-shirt dance with abandon next to a girl sporting a half-shaved head and more piercings than I could count. Nobody was judging, nobody was laughing - everyone was just... free.

The music was alien: inhuman vocals, impossible beats, and bass that shook your bones. Nothing like my old hip-hop. This stuff *changed* you.

Without thinking, I began to move. Gone was the self-conscious teenager, replaced by someone - something - else entirely. I was lost in the beat, working myself harder and harder until I felt half-hypnotized. My body was alive, electric, as if my nerves were reaching out to grasp the universe itself.

And then, in the midst of my awkward flailing, I felt a hand on my arm. Rachel, her face flushed and grinning, pulled me closer. "You're hilarious when you dance!" she shouted over the music, her eyes sparkling with amusement and something else... affection?

For a moment, I felt embarrassed, but then I saw the joy in her face. She wasn't mocking me; she was genuinely entertained. So I let loose, exaggerating my clumsy moves, reveling in her laughter. As we danced, I couldn't help but notice how she stayed close, her small frame protected by my larger one in the surging crowd.

The night wore on, and I found myself talking to strangers as if they were old friends. There was Mark, a computer geek who could barely make eye contact in the daylight but was now enthusiastically explaining the intricacies of the sound system. And Sarah, a quiet girl from my English class who I'd never heard speak more than two words, was now passionately discussing her dreams of becoming a DJ.

I looked over at Eddie, his face lit up with a grin I hadn't seen in years. Even Rachel, always so put-together and focused on her studies, seemed to have let her guard down.

It hit me then - this wasn't just about the music. It was about finding your people. In the bright lights and low bass, we'd all found a place where we could be the loudest, weirdest, most authentic versions of ourselves.

We stumbled out at dawn. Across the street, a church let out. Clean families in their Sunday best. Us, sweaty and messed up from our own twisted prayer meeting.

It struck me then how far I'd strayed from my childhood faith. I remembered the countless Sundays spent in church, the comforting rituals, the sense of community. Somewhere along the way, I'd lost that connection, that feeling of being part of something larger than myself.

But standing there, watching the churchgoers file out as our rave family dispersed, I felt a stirring in my soul. The music I'd experienced that night had awakened something in me - a hunger for connection, for transcendence, for that same sense of unity I'd once found in those church pews.

As Rachel, Eddie, and I made our way home, exhausted but exhilarated, I couldn't shake the feeling that my life had changed. The collective energy of the crowd, the euphoria of losing myself in the music - it all felt like a form of worship. The rave had become my new sanctuary, the DJ booth my pulpit, and the rhythm my prayer.

Rachel's laughter echoed in my dreams, her enjoyment of my awkward dancing a warm glow in my chest. I knew she saw me as a friend, a protector, but maybe... just maybe... there could be something more. She always said I made her feel "safe."

Little did I know the profound impact this night would have on my future - the heights it would take me to, and the depths to which it would eventually plunge me. But in that moment, basking in the afterglow of my first rave, all I felt was an overwhelming sense of possibility and the intoxicating rush of finally, truly belonging somewhere.

In the coming months and years, I would test the limits of this new world, and discover just how transformative - and potentially destructive - true devotion could be. But for now, as sleep claimed me, all I knew was that I had found my tribe, and everything was about to change.

As I fell asleep, I heard a strange sound. It was very quiet, like a deep swelling coming from underground. I thought it was just music from earlier, still in my head. I didn't know then that this weird sound would be the start of a big adventure. This adventure would test how strong I was, both in my mind and in my heart.

Chapter 3:

"Little Fluffy Clouds"

by The Orb

[105 BPM]

The rave had left a mark on my senses. As I lay in bed, trying to sleep, my mind raced with vivid daydreams. The pulsating intelligent light show and thunderous breakbeats from the night before had awakened something within me - a heightened awareness of the world's hidden rhythms.

I gave up on sleep and decided to walk it off at Riverfront Park and grab a bite.

As Rachel and I said our goodbyes after brunch, just before she headed to her Cryptography class, I found it impossible not to notice how her car door slammed in perfect sync with the song playing on her radio.Was it coincidence, or was I just more aware to the beats around me?

The park was alive with the symphony of a summer day. Children's laughter echoed in in sync bursts, their feet pattering on the concrete in time with a nearby street musician's guitar. Even the leaves rustling in the breeze seemed to whisper a melody.

I caught myself unconsciously nodding my head to the rhythm of my footsteps. The world had become my dance floor, and every sound was a potential track waiting to be mixed.

As I approached the Spokane River, the roar of the rapids hit me like a wall of sound. But instead of chaos, I heard patterns - nature's own drum machine. The rushing water created a steady bass line, while the splashing against rocks added staccato hits. I closed my eyes, letting the mist caress my face, and I swear I could almost hear a melody forming.

My mind drifted back to the Masonic Temple nearby, to the DJ who had commanded the crowd with such ease. I imagined myself in his place, thousands of dancers moving to my beat. But it wasn't just fame or recognition. It was about tapping into this newfound connection between music and life itself.

A jogger passed by, her ponytail swinging in perfect 4/4 time. A skateboard clattered nearby, its wheels creating a rhythm that would make any hip-hop producer jealous. Even the distant sound of traffic formed a sort of urban ambient track.

"I'm going to be a DJ," I said aloud, my voice mixing with the sounds of the park. But the thought didn't stop there. Why limit myself?

As if in response, a car drove by, its radio blaring. I recognized Johnny Styles' voice, cocky and self-assured. Could I do that too? Command the airwaves and the dance floor?

"Sure, why not?" I answered without hesitation. "I know music as well as any of these guys!"

In that moment, I saw my future unfold. I wasn't just going to be a DJ - I was going to be a force in both worlds. Radio and club. Turntables and microphones. I'd juggle them all, creating a symphony of my own making.

As I made my way back through the park, every sound seemed to confirm my epiphany. The click of a bicycle's gears changing. The rhythmic squeak of a swing set. The melodic call of an ice cream truck in the distance. It was all music, waiting to be harnessed.

I spotted Rachel's car pulling up, right on time. As I approached, I noticed how her fingers tapped on the steering wheel, perfectly in sync with her car's turn signal. I smiled, realizing that this newfound awareness wasn't just about becoming a DJ. It was about tuning into the rhythm of life itself.

As I slipped into the passenger seat, **Rachel** gave me a curious look. "You seem different," she said, her voice adding another layer to the ambient track of the moment.

```
def decode_signal():
# Decoding transmission...
```

INCOMING TRANSMISSION[1]

01110100 01101000 01101001 01110011 00100000 01101001
01110011 00100000 01100010 01101001 01100111 01100111 01100101
01110010 00100000 01110100 01101000 01100001 01101110 00100000
01111001 01101111 01110101 00100000 01100001 01101110 01100100
00100000 01101101 01100101

location_data = https://maps.app.goo.gl/uWJrh1hozCviK9Xf9
Communication_data = https://forms.gle/cNDJnr3usK2h38b87
signal = **"68747470733a2f2f6269742e6c792f334162243346445"** # Hex for

```
return bytes.fromhex(signal).decode('utf-8')
# Signal lost. [End Transmission]
```

As Rachel and I said our goodbyes after brunch, just before she headed to her Cryptography class, I couldn't help but notice how her car door slammed in perfect sync with the song playing on her radio.

I grinned, feeling the beat of my heart align with the idle of the car's engine. "I am different," I replied. "I think I've found my calling."

---

1.   https://maps.app.goo.gl/uWJrh1hozCviK9Xf9

Little did I know, as we drove away from Riverfront Park, that this was just the first beat of a much larger track - one that would take me to heights I never imagined, and depths I never expected. But at that moment, all I could hear was the promise of music ahead.

Chapter 4:

"Hits From The Bong" by Cypress Hill

[92 BPM]

When I walked into 97.3 "The X" FM, I was hit with a visual assault that made me question if I'd stumbled into a "Before" photoshoot for a personal grooming infomercial. The walls were plastered with photos of people I'd only known as disembodied voices, and let me tell you, there was a reason they were on the radio.

These guys looked like they'd been pulled straight from the back row of every high school classroom - the kind who treated personal hygiene as an opt-out program and considered headbanging a form of morning exercise. Long, unkempt hair, faces that had never met a razor, and clothes that seemed to have survived a metal concert mosh pit and lost. I half expected to see "Missing" posters for their fashion sense.

"So this is where the smokers' alley graduates end up," I muttered, then realized with a sinking feeling that these audio ogres had one massive advantage over me - experience. Years of it. While I'd been busy trying to figure out which end of a pencil to use in college, these guys had been honing their craft, turning their voices into the dulcet tones that caressed Spokane's eardrums nightly.

I smoothed out my mismatched thrift store suit. It wasn't much, but it was all I could afford on my tight budget. Despite the cheap polyester, I felt confident. Maybe the program director would see past my outfit and recognize my potential as an eager rookie.

"Mr. Styles will be right with you," the secretary chirped, eyeing my fidgeting hands as I checked my watch for the umpteenth time. "He's always really busy, you understand. Nervous?"

"Me? Nah, I'm chill," I lied through my teeth, my leg jittering like it was trying to morse code an SOS.

She smirked, giving me a once-over. "Relax, kid. That suit's straight out of your old man's closet, isn't it? It'll score you points with the big man. He's got a soft spot for vintage polyester."

I felt my face burn hotter than a faulty transistor radio and buried my nose in a trade magazine, pretending to be fascinated by an article on the riveting world of FCC regulations.

Suddenly, the hallway erupted with the sound of laughter that could wake the dead - or at least the demographics that "The X" was desperately trying to reach. It was the voice of legend, the man who put the "style" in Styles - Johnny himself, Spokane's answer to Howard Stern and the bane of every parent's existence.

On air, Johnny was a force of nature, a category five hurricane of snark and sass. His show was a nightly bloodbath of egos, where callers came to request songs and left with emotional scars and therapy bills. This was the guy who made a twelve-year-old cry on air for daring to request Billy Ray Cyrus during a Metallica song. The crowd ate it up like it was auditory crack, and Johnny served it with a side of "I do NOT care."

"Oh, that's him now," the secretary said, rising from her desk. "Just got back from 'lunch.' I'll let him know you're here."

I swallowed hard, hoping against hope that Johnny's on-air persona was just that - a persona. Because if not, I was about to walk into the lion's den wearing Kibbles 'n Bits underwear.

"Who? What? Aaron, huh?" Johnny's voice boomed from behind his closed door, making the gold records on the wall vibrate. "Yeah, yeah. Hang on a minute."

The door swung open, and there he stood - Johnny Styles in the flesh, looking like he'd just rolled out of bed and into a pile of CDs. "You Aaron?" he asked, barely glancing at me as he shuffled through a stack of singles.

"Y-yes, sir," I stammered, jumping to my feet like I'd been electrocuted.

"Sit down. I'll be with you soon," he grunted, disappearing back into his office with a slam that made me wonder if the door was reinforced to withstand his daily mood swings.

The secretary offered me a sympathetic smile and a doughnut. I declined, my stomach doing somersaults that would make an Olympic gymnast jealous.

Forty-five minutes and three re-reads of "Billboard's Top 100 Ways to Alienate Your Audience" later, Johnny emerged, looking surprised to see me still there, like I was a piece of furniture he'd forgotten about.

"You still here? Forgot you were waiting. Want a doughnut?"

"No, thank you," I replied, wondering if this was some sort of weird hazing ritual.

"Your loss, partner. I'll be right back," he said, heading for the exit.

Something in me snapped. Maybe it was the hunger, maybe it was the nerves, or maybe it was the realization that I was one "no, thank you" away from being forever known as "that doughnut guy" at KXXS.

"Sir," I blurted, surprising myself with my boldness, "I've been waiting for over an hour and a half. I'm not here for pastries or to memorize trade magazines. I'm here for an internship. Can you spare five minutes? I promise I'll make it as painless as possible - for both of us."

Johnny turned, fixing me with a stare that could peel paint. Finally, he spoke.

"I was gonna buy that exact same jacket at the thrift store the other day," he smirked. "Guess I dodged a bullet there, huh?"

He ushered me into his office, a shrine to rock 'n' roll excess and questionable interior decorating choices. Gold records competed for wall space with autographed photos of music legends. I had to stifle a laugh when I spotted a framed picture of Johnny shaking hands with Billy Ray Cyrus - the same Billy Ray he'd made a pre-teen cry over on air.

Johnny slouched behind his desk, eyeing my resume like it was written in hieroglyphics. "So," he drawled, "says here you've got jack squat to offer this station. Am I supposed to be impressed by your extensive experience in... what's this? 'Professional nap-taking 101'?"

I opened my mouth, ready to defend my admittedly sparse qualifications, when Johnny did something that made me question if I'd accidentally wandered onto the set of a Cheech and Chong movie. With his left hand, he lit an incense stick. With his right, he casually unrolled a baggie of what was definitely not oregano.

"Fresh from the college scene, huh?" he said, his fingers deftly rolling a joint that would make Willie Nelson proud. "Think you've got what it takes to hang with the big boys? What can you offer me that I can't get from any other snot-nosed kid with dreams of being the next Casey Kasem?"

I watched, mesmerized, as he licked the paper, sealing it with the precision of a master craftsman. My brain screamed at me to say something - anything - but my mouth felt like it was full of cotton.

"I, uh... I believe I can handle whatever you throw at me," I finally managed, my eyes still glued to the joint as Johnny lit up, filling the office with a sweet, pungent aroma. "Just like the rest of you... fellas."

Johnny took a long drag, holding the smoke in his lungs before exhaling slowly. "What do you wanna be, some superstar DJ? 'Cause we don't do that here. No room for wannabe shock jocks or pretty boys looking to get laid. Let me tell you something, kid. Ninety percent of our female listeners are living proof that you can't judge a book by its cover - or a voice by its owner. They all sound like phone sex operators, but trust me, reality's a bitch."

He took another hit, then held the joint out to me. "Want a toke?"

I stared at the offered joint, my mind racing. Here I was, standing on the precipice of my dream career, and the price of admission was apparently a hit off the devil's lettuce. I'd never so much as looked at weed before, let alone smoked it. But as I watched the smoke curl lazily towards the ceiling, I made a decision that would change the course of my life.

I reached out and took the joint.

As I hacked and wheezed, trying to play it cool while my lungs staged a revolt, Johnny's eyes narrowed. He leaned forward, cocking his head like a curious dog.

"Hold up," he said, reaching over to turn up the radio on his desk. The smooth beats of Beastie Boys filled the room. "Say something."

"What do you want me to say?" I asked, my voice rough from coughing.

Johnny waved his hand impatiently. "Anything, just talk."

I cleared my throat, desperately trying to think of something clever. My eyes landed on the Billy Ray Cyrus photo, and suddenly, the words just flowed.

"Well," I began, unconsciously matching the rhythm of the song, "I guess you could say I'm just an achy breaky heart looking for my place in radio. But unlike Billy Ray's mullet, I promise I won't be a passing trend."

Johnny's eyebrows shot up, a grin spreading across his face. "Well, well, well. Look who's got jokes and rhythm. Keep going."

I continued, my words falling in sync with Snoop's laid-back flow. "I may look like I raided my grandpa's closet, but don't let the polyester fool you. I've got a voice that can make drive-time traffic sound like a party and the morning zoo feel like Woodstock."

As I spoke, I noticed Johnny's head bobbing slightly to the beat, his fingers tapping on the desk. He was listening, really listening, in a way he hadn't been before.

"I'm here to turn dials and blow minds," I continued, riding the wave of sudden confidence. "To make the airwaves sizzle and the ratings soar. Because let's face it, radio needs a real voice. And that voice? It's gonna be mine."

I finished just as the song faded out, leaving the office in a moment of stunned silence. Johnny stared at me, his joint forgotten and smoldering between his fingers.

"Well, I'll be damned," he said finally, shaking his head in disbelief. "You look like you should be doing my taxes, but you sound like you belong behind a mic. And that rhythm... it's like you've got a metronome for a heartbeat."

He leaned back in his chair, regarding me with new interest. "You know, most kids come in here thinking they're God's gift to the radio because they can string two sentences together without drooling. But you... there's something different about you, Dookster."

I tried not to let my surprise show. Had I actually impressed the great Johnny Styles?

"Don't get me wrong," Johnny continued, stubbing out the joint. "You're still greener than Kermit the Frog's ass, and that suit is an affront to fashion everywhere. But that voice of yours... it's got potential. And how did you pick up that beat? That's not something you can teach."

He stood up, circling his desk to stand in front of me. "Here's the deal, kid. I'm not promising you anything. But I'm willing to give you a shot. A small one. You'll start at the bottom - I'm talking 3 AM weather reports and PSAs about the dangers of toe fungus. But if you work hard, keep your mouth shut when it needs to be shut, and prove to me that what I just heard wasn't a fluke... well, who knows?"

I was floating, barely able to contain my excitement. "Thank you, Mr. Styles. I promise you won't regret this."

Johnny snorted. "Oh, I'm sure I will. Multiple times. But that's showbiz, baby." He clapped my shoulder, almost knocking me. "Now get out of here before I change my mind. And Dookster?"

I turned back, my hand on the doorknob. "Yes, sir?"

"Burn that suit. You look like a disco ball threw up on a scarecrow."

As I left the office, my head spinning from more than just the secondhand smoke, I couldn't help but grin. I had just landed my first radio gig. It wasn't much, but it was a start. And in this business, sometimes all you need is a foot in the door - even if that foot is wearing a secondhand loafer.

Little did I know, this was only the start of a wild ride that would take me to the heights of radio stardom and the depths of the underground rave scene. But for now, I had a mission: find a new suit, practice my 3 AM voice, and figure out how to make toe fungus sound exciting.

The Spokane airwaves would never, ever, be the same.

Chapter 5:

"Gonna Make You Sweat"

by C & C Music Factory

[112 BPM]

The oversized ears of the Easter bunny costume drooped before me, a ridiculous symbol of how far I'd fallen. Once a wide-eyed radio station hopeful, now a furry holiday mascot. The irony wasn't lost on me – here I was, living my dream of working in radio, and I felt more like an outcast than ever.

"No way," I muttered, pushing the costume away. "I didn't drop out of college for this, Johnny."

Johnny Styles, the self-proclaimed "big boy" of radio, fixed me with a hard stare. "Listen, kid. You want to make it in this business? Sometimes you gotta swallow your pride and do the dirty work. Or are you too good for that?"

His words stung, striking at the heart of my inner conflict. I wanted fame, recognition, to be more than just Aaron from Spokane. But at what cost? I glanced at the Masonic Temple looming in the distance, its weathered facade a silent witness to my struggle.

With a heavy sigh, I reached for the costume. As I slipped it on, a strange warmth spread through my body, starting from my chest and radiating outward. I dismissed it as claustrophobia, but a small part of me wondered if it was something more.

The warmer-than-average spring sun beat down mercilessly as I shuffled through Riverfront Park, my hairy knees peeking out from beneath the ill-fitting fur. Despite my initial resistance, a spark flickered in my chest. Kids pointed and waved, their faces lighting up at the sight of the seven foot white rabbit.

"Ladies and gentlemen, feast your eyes on the newest addition to our KXXX family!" Johnny's voice thundered through the speakers. "It's the Easter Bunny himself! And would you look at that - seems like somebunny's been eating their carrots! This rabbit's practically a Harlem Globetrotter!"

I grimaced beneath the mask, but something made me wave enthusiastically. The children's laughter was infectious, and I was now getting into the spirit of things.

As the Easter egg hunt began, I watched the kids scatter across the park. Some eggs were hidden in plain sight, their pastel colors gleaming in the sunlight. Others were tucked away in shadowy corners, requiring more determined searching. It struck me as a perfect metaphor for life – sometimes joy is right in front of us, other times we have to look harder to find it.

A soft sobbing caught my attention. A little girl stood alone, her basket empty while other children raced past with armfuls of eggs. Without thinking, I lumbered over to her.

"Hey there," I said, my voice muffled by the mask. "What's wrong?"

"I can't find any eggs," she sniffled, looking up at me with tear-filled eyes.

I knelt down, ignoring the sweat trickling down my back. "Well, let's look together, shall we?"

We set off, searching the nooks and crannies of the park. As we hunted, I was genuinely enjoying the moment. There was something pure about helping this child, a far cry from the selfish ambition that had driven me lately.

"Look!" I exclaimed, pointing to a glowing egg nestled in the hollow of a tree. The girl's face lit up as she reached for it, and I felt an inexplicable sense of joy wash over me.

A high-pitched squeal cut our egg-hunting adventure short. "MOMMY! Look, the Easter bunny!"

Before I could react, a tiny blonde missile launched herself at my legs, wrapping her arms around my thighs with surprising strength. Her parents cooed, fumbling with a disposable camera.

"Can we get a picture?" the dad asked, grinning. "In the shade, maybe?"

"Shade," I thought desperately. "Sweet, sweet shade."

I stumbled towards a cluster of lilac trees, the children still clinging to me. My vision swam, darkness creeping in at the edges. The strange warmth I'd felt earlier intensified, becoming almost unbearable.

The last thing I heard was Johnny's voice over the speakers: "Looks like our furry friend is feeling a little hot under the collar! Maybe he needs a cold drink – or a litter box!"

Then, everything went black.

I came to moments later, sprawled on the ground. The little girl's flowered overalls were covered in a technicolor mess of my stomach contents. Her wails pierced the air as her horrified parents whisked her away.

"Holy cow, folks!" Johnny's voice crackled over the PA. "Looks like the Easter Bunny had a little too much jellybean juice! Our furry friend is hopping off to sleep it off, but don't worry - he'll be back next year, hopefully with a stronger stomach! This is Johnny Styles saying 'Happy Easter, Spokane!'"

"Dookie the Pukey Bunny," I muttered, peeling off the sweat-soaked mask. "Add that to the list of nicknames I never wanted."

As I sat in the air-conditioned station van later, contemplating the disaster, Johnny sauntered over. He leaned against the open door, a smirk playing on his lips.

"You did good out there, kid," he said, surprising me. "Not everyone can take the heat – literally or figuratively."

I looked up at him, unsure if this was just another jab.

"This business isn't for the faint of heart," Johnny continued. "You gotta be willing to make a fool of yourself, to push through the embarrassment. Heck, I've done worse things than throw up on a kid to get where I am."

He tossed me a cold bottle of water. "You survived your first trial by fire. Or should I say, trial by fur? Get some rest, Dook. Tomorrow, we see what else you're made of."

As Johnny walked away, I wondered: was this the beginning of my rise in radio, or just another cosmic joke at my expense? The warmth I'd felt in the costume lingered, a reminder that something strange was at play. Either way, I had a feeling my journey was far from over.

I thought about the little girl I'd helped, the brief moment of pure joy I'd experienced. It was a far cry from the fame and recognition I craved, but there was something to it – a glimmer of light in the shadows of my ambition.

As I closed my eyes, the image of the glowing egg in the hollow tree stayed with me, a beacon of hope in the uncertain path ahead.

Chapter 6:

"Fantastic Voyage" by Coolio

[102 BPM]

The ice pack dribbled down my blistered face as I sprawled on the couch, practically bathing in Crystal Light. The cool air conditioning was a contrast to the sweltering heat in the claustrophobic costume. My mind wandered, conjuring up big visions of my newfound status.

"I am a radio broadcasting network's awkward bunny boy!" I declared to the empty room. "I fear no man, for I am now a vital part of society! If anyone gets in the way of my destiny and dreams... why, I'll either defecate or project vomit on my detractors!"

The silence that followed my proclamation was broken by the harsh ring of the telephone. I reached for it, grimacing at the movement.

"Yellow?" I replied, trying to sound cooler than I felt.

"Bunny! We are going for a ride." Eddie's voice crackled through the receiver. "I don't want no moaning' or griping'. It's time to take the furry man out on a mission for some hippity-hoppity fun." **

I couldn't help but grin. Eddie always seemed to materialize with plans when boredom threatened. "What've you got in mind?"

"Well," Eddie drawled, his voice tinged with mischief, "I may or may not have stumbled upon a flyer for this new joint called 'Club OZ'. All ages, hip-hop DJ... Could be our ticket out of Dullsville tonight."

I chuckled. "How do you always manage to find these things, Ed? Got some kind of radar for teenage debauchery?"

"What can I say?" Eddie's laugh held a hint of something darker. "When the old man is in the hospital so much, you get creative with your free time."

In that brief moment, the unspoken burden of Eddie's home life lingered between us, creating a familiar tension in the air.

Eddie's dark humor was a way of coping with the mess life had dealt him.

Losing his parents at three, and with his grandpa in a nursing home, Eddie had free run of the trailer he grew up in. But instead of enjoying the freedom, he seemed lost in the empty space. I could see the desperation behind his frenetic energy, the way he filled the silence with loud music and a revolving door of sketchy people.

Maybe this party was Eddie's way of feeling less alone in that too-quiet trailer, even if just for one night.

I cleared my throat, pushing past it. "So, this OZ place. Sounds intriguing. What's the deal?"

"All-ages club, man. DJ goes by 'Nexus' or something. Probably thinks he's hot stuff." Eddie's voice perked up. "Could be fun to check out, yeah? Better than cruising the strip for the millionth time."

I glanced at my reflection in the TV screen, wincing at my still-reddened face. "I don't know, Ed. I'm not exactly looking my best after the whole... bunny incident."

"Oh, come on!" Eddie groaned. "You can't let one little egg-tossing episode keep you down. Besides," his voice took on a sly tone, "I heard through the online boards that Rachel might be there."

My heart paused a beat at the mention of her name. "Rachel? You sure?"

"As sure as my killer hangover tomorrow," Eddie quipped. "So, you in or what?"

After a brief pause, a surge of resolve coursed through me. "Yeah, alright. Let's do it. Pick me up in an hour?"

"You got it, boss. Oh, and Aaron?"

"Yeah?"

"Try not to hurl on anyone this time, yeah?"

I rolled my eyes, hanging up as Eddie's laughter echoed through the phone. As I headed to the shower, I couldn't shake the excitement and nervousness bubbling in my stomach. A night out in Spokane's thriving (ha!) teenage scene. What could possibly go wrong?

———

The bass of Ice Cube filled the air as Eddie and I approached The OZ. The converted dance studio looked almost unrecognizable, its windows blacked out and a line of teenagers snaking down the block.

"Man, check out these wannabe ballers," Eddie muttered, eyeing the crowd. "Looks like Tommy Hilfiger and FUBU had a clearance sale at the mall."

I nodded, trying to appear nonchalant as we joined the line. "Yeah, and is that... is that guy wearing a clock around his neck?"

Eddie snickered. "Flavor Flav wannabe. Bet it's his dad's alarm clock spray-painted gold."

We shuffled forward, taking in the sea of baggy jeans, oversized jerseys, and chunky gold chains that were probably more cubic zirconia than actual bling. The air was thick with cheap Bod Man cologne and the unmistakable scent of desperation to be cool.

"You gotta admit though," I said, "some of them are pulling it off. That girl over there? She looks like she stepped right out of a TLC video."

Eddie's eyes widened. "Dude, that's Sarah from Bio class. Since when did she get so... fly?"

I shrugged, suddenly feeling very underdressed in my thrift store flannel and worn jeans. "Maybe we should've shoplifted ShopKo for some parachute pants or something."

"Speak for yourself," Eddie grinned, adjusting his backwards cap. "I'm straight outta Compton... by way of K-Mart." We both laughed, our nervousness easing a bit as we inched closer to the club's entrance.

As we approached, the scent of incense wafted out, a sharp difference from the typical teen club smell of sweat and hormones. It was a subtle hint of the unique atmosphere that awaited us inside.

We paid our cover and entered the dimly lit club. The transformation from dance studio to teenage nightclub was impressive, if a bit amateur. Black fabric draped the mirrors, and strobes flashed across the dance floor. But there was something else, an intangible quality that set this place apart.

That something was Nexus.

I'd heard whispers about him around school - the Lewis & Clark High graduate who threw the hottest house parties, now turning this old dance hall into the hottest teen spot in Spokane. As my eyes adjusted to the darkness, I saw him behind the decks, and suddenly, those rumors made sense.

Nexus moved with a fluid grace, his bare feet tapping out rhythms on the worn wooden floor of the DJ booth. His hands danced over the turntables, but his eyes - they were constantly scanning the crowd, connecting with dancers, encouraging the wallflowers with a smile and a nod.

"Dude," I whispered to Eddie, "he's barely even looking at the equipment. How's he doing that?"

Eddie shrugged, equally mesmerized. "M-magic, man. *Magic.*"

As we made our way through the crowd, I noticed how Nexus's energy seemed to infect everyone around him. Even the most awkward dancers moved with a newfound confidence, swept up in the music and the DJ's unwavering positivity.

That's when I spotted a familiar figure near the DJ booth. My heart leapt into my throat.

Rachel.

She was leaning against the booth, laughing at something Nexus was saying. The way the lights played off her hair, the curve of her smile... I was transfixed.

Eddie nudged me. "There's your girl, man. Go talk to her!"

I swallowed hard, suddenly feeling like that awkward kid in math class again. "I... I don't know, Ed. She looks busy."

"Don't be a wuss," Eddie scoffed. "You're the radio star now, remember? Go work that magic."

I made my way to the booth. Rachel turned as I approached, her eyes widening in recognition.

"Aaron?" She had to raise her voice over the music. "I didn't expect to see you here!"

I tried for a casual grin, probably looking more constipated than cool. "Yeah, well, you know me. Always up for a good time."

Rachel laughed, the sound making my stomach do backflips. "Right, because you're such a party animal. How'd you even hear about this place?"

I jerked a thumb towards Eddie. "My personal social secretary. He's got a nose for these things."

"I bet," **Rachel** smirked. She turned to Nexus, who was watching our interaction with amusement. "Oh! Aaron, this is Nexus. Nexus, this is Aaron. He's a DJ on The X!"

def send_signal():

 # >> Sending signal...

TARGETING

01110100 01101000 01101001 01110011 00100000 01110111 01100001 01110011 00100000 01110100 01101000 01100101 00100000 01101110 01101001 01100111 01101000 01110100 00100000 01110111 01101000 01100101 01110010 01100101 00100000 01110100 01101000 01101001 01101110 01100111 01110011 00100000 01100011 01101000 01100001 01101110 01100111 01100101 01100100

encoded_link = https://bit.ly/3yR9ZCc

cross_reference = https://crosswordlabs.com/embed/life-remixed

return encoded_link

 # Signal interrupted. [Transmission Cut]

Nexus's eyes lit up with recognition. "Wait. As in, the Easter Bunny radio guy from the news?"

I felt my face flush. "Uh, yeah. That's... that's me."

To my surprise, Nexus laughed, but there was no malice in it. "Man, that's wild! I gotta say, you've got some guts showing your face after that. Respect." He reached out, clasping my hand in a warm handshake. "I hear you're getting into the DJ game. That true?"

I nodded, suddenly feeling at ease in Nexus's presence. "Yeah, I just started at the station. Still learning the ropes, you know?"

Nexus's smile grew. "We all start somewhere." Tell you what, stick around after my set. I'll show you a few tricks."

Before I could respond, a commotion near the entrance caught our attention. The energy in the room shifted palpably, like a storm cloud rolling in over a sunny day.

"Make way for the real star!" a voice shouted over the music. "DJ Havok's in the house!"

I watched a guy in sunglasses and spiky blond hair, carrying a crate of records, pushed his way through the crowd. Rachel's eyes lit up, her attention immediately drawn to the newcomer. The pit in my stomach grew as I realized I'd lost her interest as quickly as I'd gained it.

As Havok made his way to the booth, nudging Nexus aside, I felt a hand on my shoulder. Eddie appeared, two girls in tow.

"Hate to break up the party," he grinned, "but I've got some ladies here who are dying to continue this shindig back at your place."

I hesitated, glancing back at Rachel, who was now hanging on Havok's every word. The sting of rejection mixed with the temptation of Eddie's offer.

"You know what?" I said, tearing my eyes from the booth. "Yeah, why not? Let's go."

As we made our way to the exit, the sound of an air raid siren broke through the music. Havok's set was beginning, and the energy in the club shifted again. Gone was the warm, inclusive vibe Nexus had cultivated. In its place was something darker, more intense.

For a moment, I paused, drawn in by the pulsing beats and the electric atmosphere. But then I saw Rachel, her eyes locked on Havok, and I knew it was time to go.

"Come on," I told Eddie and the girls. "The night's still young."

Venturing into Spokane's crisp night, a profound change enveloped me, altering the atmosphere. Whether it was the music, the glimpse into this new world, or the ache of watching Rachel slip away, I knew one thing for certain:

Life was about to take uncharted and unpredictable turns.

And somewhere in the back of my mind, I heard Nexus's words echoing: "I'll show you a few tricks." Little did I know how prophetic those words would prove to be, or how deeply they would shape the path that lay ahead of me.

** **Footnote:** 0:52-1:04

Chapter 7:

"Standing Outside a Broken Phone Booth with Money in My Hand" by Primitive Radio Gods

[95 BPM]

The world spun like a warped record as Eddie and I sprawled on the bathroom floor, our bodies heavy as lead. The cool tiles offered little relief from the pounding in our skulls. Our eyes met, bloodshot and bleary, a silent understanding passing between us.

"Yo, Ed," I groaned, my mouth feeling like I'd swallowed a desert. "Tell me we didn't try to outdrink a frat house last night."

Eddie's response came out slow and thick, his stutter more pronounced than usual. "W-worse. We tried to out-dance a g-glowstick army. My legs feel like overcooked s-spaghetti."

"Ugh. Next time, just let me pick a fight with a bouncer. It'll hurt less in the morning."

The phone's sudden ring pierced our eardrums like a needle on vinyl. We both winced, the sound amplifying our misery.

"Not it," Eddie mumbled, burying his face in a threadbare towel.

"Voicemail's got it," I groaned, silently willing the ringing to stop.

To our surprise, a feminine giggle floated through the door, followed by, "You boys decent in there?"

Confusion cut through my fog. "Thought they bailed..."

The brunette's voice continued, tinged with amusement. "Some lady called for Aaron.

Told her there's no Aaron here, just Dookie, and he's... occupied. She hung up real quick!"

My stomach dropped. "Eddie! My mom!"

As if on cue, the phone on the wall rattled. I fumbled to answer it, nearly braining myself on the sink.

"Hello?"

"Dook." Johnny's gruff voice sent a chill down my backside. "You are needed at the station. ASAP."

"But-"

"I'll give you like, thirty minutes. It's really important. I gotta go."

The line went dead.

Adrenaline surged through me, momentarily masking the hangover. "Everybody out!" I bellowed, launching into frantic motion. "Eddie, lock up! Ladies, the party's over!"

I tore through the house, grabbing essentials: Pepto, hat, keys. A quick sniff of my shirt made me recoil. "Screw it," I muttered, dousing myself in Old Spice.

The cool night air hit me as I revved up my trusty Power Wagon, my stomach lurching with each pothole. Streetlights blurred into streaks of neon, the city a kaleidoscope of sound and color. By some miracle, I made it to the station without becoming roadkill.

Stumbling out of the elevator, I struggled with the keys, my hands refusing to cooperate. Johnny's face appeared in the crack of the door, his expression of disgust and amusement.

"You're late," he growled, ushering me inside.

The control room loomed before me, a labyrinth of buttons and dials. Johnny's face was a mask of irritation and amusement.

"Listen up, Dookster," he growled. "The overnight guy showed up wasted. Had ten minutes of dead air while he took a little nap between CDs. I kicked his sorry ass out. Now you're up."

The irony wasn't lost on me. Here I was, barely sobered up, replacing a guy who was too drunk to work. I swallowed hard, tasting the lingering hints of tonight's poor decisions.

Johnny pointed around the room. "CDs are there, program log is here. The EBS tone button is under the table. Keep us on air, you keep your job. Simple as that."

He ushered me towards the control board. "Don't mess this up, kid."

With that, Johnny slammed the door, leaving me alone with the behemoth of equipment. Panic rose in my throat as I noticed the CD player's countdown: twenty seconds left.

My eyes darted frantically between the fading song and the sea of controls. Sweat beaded on my forehead as I identified the crucial buttons: recorder, microphone, CD 2. The room swam a little, my hangover battling with adrenaline.

Three. Two. One.

I jabbed at what I hoped was the right button, screwing my eyes shut. The smooth transition of one song into another filled the room. I exhaled, not realizing I'd been holding my breath.

As the adrenaline ebbed, the reality of my situation sank in. I, hungover and barely functional, was now responsible for keeping KXXS on air. The pressure mounted with each passing second, the irony of the situation not lost on me. Here I was, a drunk replacing a drunk, fumbling through one of the biggest opportunities of my life.

An hour into my impromptu shift, a flashing red light caught my eye. The computer screen demanded an EBS test. My heart rate skyrocketed. I'd heard about these, knew they were FCC mandated, but had no clue how to actually do one.

The intro began to play automatically: "This is a test of the Emergency Broadcast System..."

Panic seized me. Where was the dang tone button? My eyes scanned the board frantically, finding nothing.

In a moment of desperation, I grabbed the mic and did the only thing I could think of. I made the tone myself.

"BeeeeEEEEeeeeeEEEEeeeeeeeeeeeeEEEEEEEEEEEEEEp..."

My voice wavered, a poor imitation of the proper tone. "This concludes our test of the Emergency Broadcast System. Had this been an actual emergency..."

I paused, a sudden burst of inspiration hitting me. "...you'd probably be better off trusting your local weatherman. At least he's right 50% of the time."

The hotline rang moments later. Johnny's laughter boomed through the receiver. "Kid, that was the worst EBS test I've ever heard. But that quip at the end? Pure gold. You might just have a future in this business after all."

At the first light of day, I pulled into my driveway, exhaustion weighing on my bones. The sight before me jolted me awake: my belongings strewn across the lawn, stuffed into garbage bags or piled haphazardly.

Eddie sat on the porch, a silent sentinel. Our eyes met, and I knew. Mom had finally made good on her threat. I'd broken the cardinal rule: no parties, no trouble, or you're out. Her remote property caretakers were swift to do her bidding from afar.

"Saved what I could," Eddie said softly.

I collapsed onto the damp grass, my choices crushing me. The rumble of an approaching truck broke the silence.

"My gramps' old hauler. Neighbor, too." Eddie explained. "Here to help move you in with us. For now."

I looked up at my best friend, gratitude and shame warring within me. As he helped me to my feet, I couldn't hold back the tears. Eddie held me for a moment before pushing me away with a gentle shove.

"Alright, alright. Enough of that sappy stuff," he said, his voice gruff but kind. "Let's get moving. You've got a new life waiting."

As we filled the truck, a profound sense of uncertainty gripped me, suggesting that this was merely the genesis of an unconventional and protracted odyssey. The rave scene, the radio gig, it all seemed to be spiraling out of control. But with Eddie by my side, maybe, just maybe, I could ride this chaotic wave.

Chapter 8:

"High and Dry" by Radiohead

[88 BPM]

The smell of old beer and moldy Godfather's Pizza boxes filled Eddie's place. I lay on his living room floor, thinking about how quickly things had changed. Just days ago, I was throwing huge parties at my mom's house. Now I was crashing at my best friend's, surrounded by his mess. It was a big step down.

Eddie's trailer had once been party central, but compared to my mom's digs, it was a dump. Funny how quickly fortunes can change. One minute you're the king of the castle, the next you're sleeping on a beer-stained shag.

A nagging voice in the back of my head reminded me that living with your best friend isn't always the dream scenario it's cracked up to be. With strangers, you can set boundaries. With old friends, those lines blur faster than a DJ's crossfade.

The whir of a vacuum cleaner jolted me from my reverie, its broken belt causing it to push debris around rather than suck it up. Eddie's voice came up through the noise. "Yo, sleeping beauty! Time to rise and shine. We've got company coming."

I groaned, shifting my aching body onto the couch. "What ungodly hour is it?"

"It's 'get your ass up o'clock,'" Eddie retorted, his usual stutter mysteriously absent. "Havok's swinging by to talk shop."

The mention of Havok's name sent an involuntary shiver through me. "Havok? That arrogant prick from The OZ? What's he want?"

Eddie killed the vacuum, his eyes darting nervously. "H-he's, uh, planning his own r-rave. Wants to t-talk strategy." The stutter was back, a tell-tale sign of Eddie's discomfort.

"Since when are you and Havok so chummy?" I probed, suddenly suspicious of their connection.

Eddie's gaze flickered away. "We j-just hit it off at the club, man. No big d-deal."

Something about Eddie's demeanor didn't sit right, but before I could press further, my mind wandered to Rachel. Beautiful, enigmatic Rachel. I hadn't heard from her since that night at The OZ. Part of me wanted to call her, to hear her voice, but another part dreaded the awkwardness, the fumbling for words.

"You should give Rachel a ring," Eddie said, as if reading my mind. "Let her know about your, uh, change in living arrangements."

I snorted. "Yeah, that'll impress her. 'Hey Rachel, guess what? I'm homeless and crashing at Eddie's. Wanna hang out in this dump?'"

Eddie's eyes narrowed. "Don't be a jerk, man. Rachel's not like that. She likes you for you, not your address."

I wanted to believe him, but my insecurities gnawed at me. Still, I reached for the phone, my heart racing as I dialed her number.

"Hello?" Rachel's voice, sultry and slightly breathless, sent a jolt through me.

"Hey, Rachel. It's Aaron."

"Aaron! What a surprise. I was just thinking about you."

My pulse quickened. "You were?"

"Mhmm," she purred. "I caught your show the other night. You sounded... different. Good different."

I couldn't tell if she was flirting or just being polite. "Thanks. I, uh, just wanted to let you know I'm not at my mom's place anymore. Got the boot for throwing too many ragers."

"Oh no," Rachel said, but there was a hint of amusement in her voice. "Where are you staying?"

"Eddie's," I admitted. "It's temporary."

There was a pause, and I could almost hear the wheels turning in Rachel's head. When she spoke again, her tone had shifted, becoming more hesitant. "Listen, Aaron... I was wondering if you're free on June 3rd. It's a Saturday."

My mind raced. Was she asking me out? "I think so. Why?"

"Well," she said, drawing out the word, "it's prom night. And I was thinking... maybe we could go together? As friends," she added quickly.

My heart soared and plummeted in the same instant. Friends. Always friends. But still, it was an opportunity. "Yeah, sure," I managed. "Sounds fun."

"Great!" **Rachel's** enthusiasm seemed genuine, if a bit forced. "I'll confirm details later, okay? I've got to run."

def secure_link():

 # >> Encrypting data stream...

FACT-CHECKING

01110111 01101000 01100101 01110010 01100101 00100000 01100100 01101001 01100100 00100000 01110101 00100000 01100111 01101111

link = https://bit.ly/4fTVrT5

return link

 # Secure connection terminated. [Link Severed]

As I hung up, my emotions were tangled and confused. Rachel wanted to go to prom with me, but as friends. Was I reading too much into it? Not enough?

My contemplation was interrupted by a pounding at the door. Havok burst in without waiting for an invitation, his presence filling the small trailer like a thundercloud.

"Well, well, well," he drawled, eyeing me with barely concealed contempt. "If it isn't the boy wonder of Spokane radio."

I bristled at his tone. "Havok. What brings you to our humble abode?"

Havok sprawled on the couch, all false bravado and sharp edges. "Business, my friend. The kind that could make us all very wealthy."

As Havok laid out his plans for "Ritual," his proposed rave, I couldn't shake the feeling that I was being pulled into something dangerous. The way Eddie hung on Havok's every word, the furtive glances they exchanged – it all screamed trouble.

Havok's eyes were unnaturally wide, his pupils dilated to pinpricks. As he spoke, his jaw worked constantly, grinding his teeth in a way that set my nerves on edge.

"So, Aaron," Havok said, fixing me with an intense stare. "You're our ticket to the big time. That radio show of yours – we need you to promote Ritual. Can you do that for us?"

I hesitated, torn between my growing dislike for Havok and my curiosity about where this new rave might lead. My first experience had been incredible, a gateway to a world I never knew existed. Part of me craved more, wanted to dive deeper into the scene.

Eddie nudged me, his eyes pleading. I remembered that I was crashing at his place, indebted to him for giving me a roof over my head. How could I refuse?

"Yeah, I suppose I could mention it on air," I said, trying to keep my voice neutral. "No promises, but I'll do what I can."

Havok's face split into a wide, manic grin. "That's my man! I knew we could count on you, Dookster. This is going to be epic!"

After I agreed to promote the rave on air, Havok's demeanor shifted. He leaned in close, his breath reeking of cigarettes and something chemical.

"You know," he said, his voice low and secretive, "I gotta hand it to you. You've got good taste in women."

My stomach clenched. "What are you talking about?"

Havok's grin widened, predatory and cruel. "Rachel. She's quite the little firecracker, isn't she?"

"You don't know her," I said, my voice tight.

He laughed, a harsh, grating sound. "Oh, but I do. We got together after The OZ. She's quite the groupie, always chasing after the next big thing."

I felt the blood drain from my face. "You're lying."

Havok shrugged, leaning back with a self-satisfied smirk. "Believe what you want, man. But take it from me, she's all about the scene. The popularity, the notoriety. Don't fool yourself into thinking you're anything special to her."

As Havok reached into his pocket, pulling out a small baggie filled with yellowish powder, my world tilted on its axis. Rachel and Havok? It couldn't be true. But a nagging voice in the back of my mind whispered that it made a sick kind of sense. Her sudden interest in me after hearing me on the radio, the prom invitation "as friends"...

"Time to celebrate our new partnership," Havok announced, dumping the contents onto the coffee table.

I stood up abruptly, my stomach churning with a toxic mix of jealousy, confusion, and disgust. "I've got to get ready for work," I mumbled, retreating towards the bathroom.

As I passed, Havok raised his hand for a high five. "Right on, big man. Don't forget – June 3rd. That's when Ritual is going down. Make sure you're free."

I slapped his hand weakly, my mind reeling. June 3rd – the night of Rachel's prom. The collision of my two worlds loomed on the horizon, and I had a sinking feeling that I was about to be caught in the crossfire.

I looked in the mirror and hardly knew who I was anymore. I felt stuck at a turning point in my life. The future was unclear, but I knew things had to change. The rave scene tempted me with fun and new experiences. But I wondered if it was worth it. Was I ready to deal with whatever came next?

As I heard Eddie and Havok's muffled voices through the bathroom door, I knew I was in too deep to back out now. The underground beat was calling, and for better or worse, I was going to answer. But Rachel's image lingered in my mind, a bittersweet reminder of what I thought I knew and what I feared I'd lost.

Chapter 9:

"Midnight in a Perfect World" by DJ Shadow

[80 BPM]

The weekend overnight shift at The X had completely wrecked my sleep schedule. After two nights of staying awake until 8 AM, it took until Wednesday to get back on track. But come Friday, it was Mini-Thins time again, just to keep my eyes open.

I worked the night shift at the radio station, from midnight to sunrise. While everyone else in Spokane slept, I was wide awake. The studio became my own little world, with its glowing equipment and humming machines. It felt way better than being the laughing stock at Sacajawea Junior High. But sometimes, the loneliness reminded me of those tough days.

The best part of my job was talking to listeners. A nurse would call on her breaks and tell me wild stories from the ER. A truck driver checked in every week from a different state, sharing his cross-country adventures. Sometimes, callers would share funny nicknames even weirder than mine." These chats made the radio come alive.**

"You're like a lighthouse keeper," the artist told me once. "Guiding us night owls through the dark."

I liked that image. It made work less lonely, more purposeful. I could pretend I was someone important, someone people actually wanted to listen to.

Not just Aaron, the awkward kid who couldn't even make it through wrestling tryouts without disaster striking.

Being a late-night DJ had its ups and downs. Sometimes things went wrong, like when the system crashed or the power went out. These scary moments reminded me of my embarrassing days in school, but at least now I could hide behind the microphone.

I got creative with how I passed the time between calls. I'd challenge myself to intro songs using only movie quotes, or try to sneak increasingly ridiculous fake band names into my patter. "That was 'Midnight Snack' by The Insomniac Hamsters," I'd say, wondering if anyone was actually paying attention. It was silly, but it felt good to make myself laugh, to be the class clown again without fear of ridicule.

The hardest part was being an "invisible DJ" - sounding wide awake at 4 AM when I was actually exhausted. I had tricks to stay alert: splashing cold water on my face, doing jumping jacks during songs, and eating sour candy for a quick energy boost. I had to do whatever it took to sound energetic on air, just like people expected.

And there was the secret life of the studio itself. Late at night, the building took on an almost haunted quality. I swear I could hear phantom footsteps in the empty hallways, or catch glimpses of movement just out of the corner of my eye.

One night, I even convinced myself I'd seen a ghost – a misty figure standing in the doorway of the production room. Turned out it was just steam from my coffee cup creating weird shadows. At least, that's what I told myself. But part of me wondered if it was something more, if the music itself was alive in some way, trying to communicate.

During my overnight shift, I'd sometimes overhear other radio stations' "off-air" moments. I caught news reporters telling inappropriate jokes during commercials when they thought their mics were off. It felt like I was seeing the secret side of radio. I even heard Johnny Styles, sounding just as arrogant when he thought no one was listening. Hearing all this made me want to be different - to be real and honest on air.

But my favorite part of the job was the music itself. In those quiet hours, I'd discover hidden gems buried deep in our library. B-sides and obscure tracks that never saw the light of day during prime time. I'd craft little musical journeys, segueing from one mood to another, imagining the soundtrack to some noir film playing out in the Spokane night.

One night, I created an amazing mix. I blended a dreamy Mazzy Star song into some spacey trip-hop, then smoothly switched to a gritty track from Stone Temple Pilots. For a few minutes, it seemed I was running the coolest underground music club ever, even though no one could see me. It was in moments like these that I really felt how powerful music can be. It can take you beyond everyday life and touch something deep inside you.

Sure, the pay was lousy and the hours were brutal. But there was something special about being the voice in the night, a companion to all the other insomniacs and dreamers out there. In those early morning hours, anything felt possible. And for a kid from Spokane with big dreams, that was everything.

As I signed off that morning, the first rays of sunlight peeking through the studio blinds, I felt strangely exhausted and exhilarated. I was starting to understand that music wasn't just about entertainment – it was a force, a language, a way to connect with people on a level beyond words. Little did I know, this realization was only just the start of the track.

** **Footnote:** Tune in

Chapter 10:

"Block Rockin Beats" by The Chemical Brothers

[109 BPM]

The weeks since I'd last spoken to Rachel felt like an eternity. Our silence hung heavy in the air, a constant reminder of the growing distance between us. I couldn't shake the gnawing feeling that I was letting something precious slip away, but my ambition whispered louder than my heart.

Ritual loomed on the horizon, coinciding with Rachel's prom night. The conflict tore at me, but I'd made my choice. This rave wasn't just another party; it was my gateway into the world I desperately wanted to be a part of. The futuristic rhythms, the swirling lights, the euphoria of a crowd moving as one – it called to me like a siren song.

"You coming or what?" Havok's impatient voice snapped me out of my wandering mind. We were parked outside Shadle Park High, the afternoon sun glinting off the hood of his beat-up Civic. A stack of freshly printed flyers sat between us, their neon colors a stark contrast to the drab school building.

I nodded, grabbing a handful as we stepped out. "Let's do this."

Havok's flyers were works of art, I had to admit. Intricate fractals and stylized lettering promised a night of transcendent music and cutting-edge DJs. As we handed them out to eager students, I felt a surge of inspiration. This was it – my chance to dive headfirst into the scene I'd only glimpsed from afar.

"Nice work, radio boy," Havok smirked as we watched a group of giggling sophomores pore over the flyer. "Looks like your local fame might actually be good for something."

I felt annoyed by Havok's half-compliment, but I kept quiet. After all, he was my way into the scene. Havok had come to Spokane from Seattle, bringing the excitement of big-city house music with him. His DJ sets were amazing - he mixed beats and melodies in ways I'd never thought possible. And man, his turntables - those Technics 1200s - I would've done anything to get my hands on them..

As the sun dipped low, we hit our usual circuit – the mall, a few coffee shops, and finally, under the cover of my fake ID, a handful of bars. Havok's easy charm and my local connections made for a potent combination. By the time we called it a night, Ritual was the talk of the town.

"Not bad, Aaron," Havok said as we cruised down Division. "You might actually have a future in this game."

I perked up at his rare praise. "Yeah? You think maybe I could get some time on the decks at Ritual?"

Havok's laugh was sharp. "Easy there, tiger. You've got a long way to go before you're ready for prime time. But keep this up, and who knows? Maybe I'll let you warm up the crowd someday."

I tried to hide my disappointment, but Havok's keen eyes caught it. His voice softened, just a touch. "Look, man. This scene... It's not just music. It's a whole world, you know? Bro. You've got to pay your dues, learn the ropes. But stick with me, and I'll show you things you never even dreamed of."

As we pulled up to my place, I hesitated before getting out. "Havok... why me? I mean, you could have your pick of helpers in this town. Why string along some radio geek?"

Havok's eyes met mine, and just then, I glimpsed something beneath his usual bravado – a flicker of genuine connection, maybe even respect. "Because, Aaron, you've got something most of these Spokane kids don't. You can hear it – the soul of the music. You just need someone to show you how to speak its language."

I nodded, a warmth spreading through my chest despite the chill night air. As I watched Havok's tail lights disappear around the corner, I felt the weight of my choice. Rachel, the prom, the life I thought I wanted – they all seemed to belong to another person, another time.

Ahead of me lay a new path, paved with pounding bass lines and infinite possibilities. I knew it wouldn't be easy. Havok was using me, sure, but I was using him too. It was a dance, intricate and potentially dangerous, but one I was determined to master.

As I drifted off to sleep that night, my dreams were filled with the phantom whine of a needle dropping on vinyl, the first notes of a track I couldn't quite grasp but knew would change everything. Somewhere in the distance, I thought I heard Rachel calling my name, but the music was too loud, too insistent.

I was crossing a threshold, and there was no turning back.

Chapter 11:

"One Headlight" by The Wallflowers

[108 BPM]

The flickering neon sign of KXXS-FM cast an eerie glow over the empty parking lot as I pulled into my usual spot for another overnight shift. The station's tower loomed above, a sentinel in the darkness, broadcasting our signal across the sleepy town of Spokane. As I walked towards the building, the weight of the crate full of CDs reminded me of the musical arsenal Johnny organized for the night ahead.

Inside, a well-worn hum of equipment greeted me. I settled into the booth, surrounded by the warm glow of VU meters and old tape recorders. It was just me and the airwaves now, a conduit between the music and the nocturnal souls of Spokane.

Johnny's words echoed in my head as I cued up the first track: "It's all about the music and not about you." Easy for him to say when every other sentence out of his mouth was "Johnny Styles here on KXXS!" But I got it. This was my apprenticeship, my dues-paying time. Two years, he'd said. Two years of overnights, of being the invisible voice in the night, before I could hope for any real recognition.

As the clock ticked towards 4 AM, that magical hour when even Johnny's iron grip on the station seemed to loosen, I felt a familiar thrill. This was my time, when the "freaks" - as the station managers called them - came out to play.

"Alright, Spokane night owls," I said into the mic, my voice a mischievous whisper. "This is Dookie, your partner in crime for the graveyard shift. Let's take a musical journey together, shall we?"

I'd push the glowing green button on the CD player, feeling the rhythm pulse through my headphones. The light of the request line started blinking almost immediately.

"Line one. You are on the air..." I answered, suppressing a yawn.

"Hey man," came a gravelly voice. "You're the only thing keeping me awake on this long-haul drive. Can you play some Nirvana?"

I smiled, reaching for the station's rack of singles. "Coming right up, road warrior. This one's for all you night drivers out there, pushing through till dawn."

As "Come As You Are" filled the airwaves, I leaned back in my chair, feeling a connection with the unseen listener somewhere out on the dark highways. This was what radio was all about - being a lifeline, a friend in the night.

The calls kept coming, each one a little spark of human connection in the early morning hours. A nurse working the late shift at Sacred Heart, requesting some energizing dance tracks. An insomniac philosophy student wanting to debate the meaning of life between songs. A lonely truck stop waitress just looking for someone to talk to about conspiracy theories between tracks.**

I juggled their requests with the mandated playlist, trying to strike a balance between being the corporate DJ and the voice these night owls seemed to crave. It was a delicate dance, one that could come crashing down with one flash of the dreaded "Bat Phone" - Johnny's silent warning system.

Between tracks, I found myself opening up more than I ever had on air. I told stories about growing up in Spokane, my dreams of making it big on the radio. I even hinted at my crush on Rachel, though I was careful never to name names.

"You know that feeling," I said softly into the mic, "when you see someone and your whole world just... stops? That's what it's like every time I see her. But hey, enough about my love life - or lack thereof. Let's get back to the music, shall we?"

As I cued up the next song, the request lit up. I was greeted off the air by an unfamiliar, but friendly tone.

"Hey there! Sorry to interrupt your show. Caught your program last night and I've been listening again tonight. You've got something special, kid. Got time for a couple questions?"

My mind raced as he proceeded to ask things about me. Was this the break I'd been waiting for? An MTV talent scout? A rival station looking to poach new talent?

"Uh, sure," I managed to stammer out. "Who am I speaking with?"

"Name's Randy. I'm with Gold Star Broadcasting. We should talk soon. Keep up the good work."

The line went dead, leaving me in a daze. I barely noticed as the song ended, scrambling to get the next track going. My head was spinning with possibilities.

As the sun began to peek over the horizon, signaling the end of my shift, I packed up my gear with a newfound energy. The monotony of the overnight gig suddenly felt like a stepping stone to something bigger.

Driving home, I found myself taking the long way, cruising past familiar landmarks. There was Riverfront Park, where I'd spent countless summer days as a kid. Mom's old house, now occupied by strangers. The Sacajawea Junior High, site of my infamous locker room incident. The Masonic Temple, the location of my first rave experience. Each place held a memory, a piece of the puzzle that had led me here.

As I pulled up outside Eddie's place, the sound of laughter and loud music filtered through the walls. With a sigh, I reached for my trusty yellow Walkman out from its fanny pack, slipping on the headphones and cranking up the volume. The familiar rhythm pulsed through me, and I felt my body start to sway, my head nodding in that comforting, almost compulsive motion.

I noticed, as I often did in moments of stress, that my rocking intensified. The chaos inside Eddie's place, the excitement of Randy's call, the possibilities and uncertainties swirling in my mind – it all translated into a physical need for rhythm, for something to anchor me.

Instead of heading inside, I recline my seat, closing my eyes and letting the music wash over me. But even as one song faded into another, I felt a restlessness creeping in. My hand moved almost of its own accord, fingers finding the dial of my Walkman.

I began to scan the frequencies, a nightly ritual that had become as natural as breathing. The AM band crackled to life, fragments of news reports and late-night commercials drifting in and out. And then, like a beacon in the static, I heard it – that familiar, gravelly voice that had become a lifeline for insomniacs and dreamers across the nation.

Art Bell.

"Good evening, listeners," his voice rumbled through my headphones. "You're tuned to Coast to Coast AM, where the unusual is usual, and the impossible is always possible."

I felt the tension in my body begin to ease, my rocking slowing to a gentle sway. Art Bell was more than just a radio host; he was a legend, a master storyteller who wove tales of the paranormal and unexplained with a sincerity that made even the most outlandish claims seem plausible.

As I listened, Art delved into a caller's account of a UFO sighting in rural Montana. His voice was soothing and contagious. This was the magic of late-night radio – the intimacy, the shared sense of wonder, the feeling that you were part of something bigger than yourself.

My mind drifted to Randy and Gold Star Broadcasting. The realization that they were connected to Art Bell's show sent a thrill through me. To be associated, even tangentially, with a radio icon like Art – it felt like a sign, a confirmation that I was on the right path.

Art's show had always fascinated me, not just for its content, but for the way he connected with his listeners. He had a gift for making each caller feel heard, for treating even the wildest stories with respect. It was a skill I aspired to, a level of connection I hoped to achieve in my own radio career.

As Art's voice washed over me, I felt my eyelids growing heavy. The rhythmic nodding of my head slowed, my breathing deepened. This was the power of radio at its finest – a voice in the darkness, a companion in the lonely hours of the night, capable of calming even the most restless of souls.

I drifted off to sleep, Art's words mingling with my dreams. Visions of mysterious lights in the sky, of hidden government facilities, of worlds beyond our own danced behind my closed eyes. But beneath it all was a steady beat, a rhythm that pulsed like a heartbeat, reminding me of the music that had brought me this far.

In that moment, suspended between waking and dreaming, I felt a sense of certainty. This was my path. Whether it led to late-night conspiracy theories or chart-topping hits, I knew that my future lay in the airwaves, in the invisible connections forged through sound and story.

As consciousness faded, one last thought flickered through my mind. Tomorrow was another night, another chance to connect, to inspire, to be that voice in the darkness for all the other misfits and dreamers out there. And maybe, just maybe, to follow in the footsteps of legends like Art Bell, creating a sanctuary of sound in the mysterious night.

** **Footnote:** Tune in

Chapter 12:

"King Of Wishful Thinking" by Go West

[108 BPM]

The fluorescent neon of NorthTown Mall buzzed overhead, casting a celebrity-worthy glow on the throng of excited shoppers. I stumbled through the food court, my eyes heavy from another sleepless night at Eddie's.

The lingering musk of Old English beer and Swisher Sweets clung to my clothes, a striking contrast to Cinnabon and the eagerness in the air.

Johnny's voice crackled through the station's Motorola flip phone, drowning out the ambient chatter. "Dookster, we need you down here ASAP. X's big celebrity singer appearance is about to start, and I'm dead on my feet."

I groaned inwardly. "Johnny, I just finished a night shift. Can't someone else—"

"Listen, kid," Johnny cut me off, his tone sharp. "This is your chance to prove you're more than just a graveyard shift DJ. Get down here and host this thing. It's not every day we get a Star Search superstar in Spokane."

The line died before I could protest further. I sighed, running a hand through my messy hair. So much for a quiet Saturday.

As I approached the massive stage set up near the mall's central fountain, I could see Johnny hunched over the sound equipment, his signature leather jacket hanging loosely on his frame. He looked up as I approached, relief washing over his haggard face.

"About time," he growled, shoving a clipboard into my hands. "Here's the rundown. Try not to butcher the intro. And for the love of it all, don't puke on anyone this time."

I winced at the memory of the Easter Bunny incident. "That was one time, Johnny. I told you, I had food poisoning—"

But Johnny was already walking away, waving dismissively. "Break a leg, Dook. Or better yet, your larynx."

Left alone with the daunting task ahead, I scanned the crowd gathering around the stage. Hundreds of screaming fans filled the area, many holding homemade signs and wearing merchandise from our mystery singer's latest tour. The energy was electric, a far cry from the usual Saturday mall crowd.

Taking a deep breath, I stepped up to the microphone. "Uh, hello Spokane!" My voice cracked embarrassingly, earning a few confused looks from the audience. "Welcome to KXXS' special live performance. I'm your host, Doo..D-d..oo —I mean, Aaron."

As I fumbled through the introduction, I could feel sweat beading on my forehead. The stage lights were unforgiving, and my sleep-deprived brain struggled to remember the carefully scripted words on the clipboard.

"We're here today to welcome a true superstar," I continued, trying to inject some enthusiasm into my voice. "A voice that has captivated the nation, a talent that—"

Suddenly, a high-pitched squeal pierced the air. The sound system had malfunctioned, sending feedback screeching through the speakers. I winced, covering my ears as the crowd recoiled. In my haste to fix the issue, I didn't notice the water bottle at my feet.

Time seemed to slow as I pitched forward, my arms flailing wildly. I crashed into the backdrop, my momentum carrying me through the thin material. As I tumbled backstage, I caught a glimpse of our mystery singer, wide-eyed and open-mouthed, as I barreled towards them.

We collided in a tangle of limbs and sequins. I found myself sprawled across the lap of one of the biggest pop stars in the country, their perfectly coiffed hair now askew, microphone rolling across the floor.

For a moment, the entire mall fell silent. Then, chaos erupted. Security guards rushed forward, fans screamed in shock and delight.

As I scrambled to my feet, face burning with embarrassment, I caught sight of the singer. To my surprise, they were laughing, brushing off their outfit with good humor.

"Ladies and gentlemen," I managed to croak into the mic I'd somehow managed to hold onto, "please enjoy this, uh, unscheduled meet and greet while we... regroup."

The rest of the event passed in a blur of awkward transitions and forced smiles. Our celebrity guest, to their credit, took it all in stride, even joking about the "flying DJ" during their performance. By the time the last note faded, I was ready to crawl into a hole and never emerge.

Slipping on the oversized station shirt, I began the task of dismantling the stage. The mall had returned to its usual Saturday bustle, my humiliation already fading into local legend.

But as I worked, I overheard snippets of conversation—people talking about the show, laughing about the "crazy DJ tackle."

Thankfully, Rachel's aversion to malls and her preference for online shopping fortunately kept her away from the chaotic mess that transpired. **

The day's events had been a rollercoaster, but as I stepped out into the fading afternoon light, I felt a strange sense of accomplishment. I'd survived, humiliation and all. And in this business, sometimes that was all you could ask for.

** **Footnote:** 0:37-0:53

Chapter 13:

"Everlong" by Foo Fighters

[79 BPM]

Rachel and I hadn't spoken for almost five weeks. Each day felt longer than the next. I tried to convince myself she was hanging out with Havok or had found a better prom date. I thought, "If she really wanted to go with me, she would've called by now." I kept telling myself this to try and feel better, but it still hurt.

Meanwhile, the buzz for Havok's upcoming party was electric. It seemed like everyone I knew was either going or planning to show up after the Lewis and Clark High School prom. I'd convinced myself that nothing, not even Rachel – the girl of my dreams – could stop me from attending this rave. It was my chance to be part of something bigger, to finally belong.

One lazy afternoon, the shrill ring of the telephone jolted me awake. Fearing it might be Johnny with another grueling assignment, I let the answering machine pick up.

"Aaron, it's Rachel..." Her voice, with a soft note of hesitation and hope, filled the room. **

My heart leapt into my throat as I scrambled off the hard floor, my stiff legs protesting as I lunged for the cordless receiver. I fumbled to turn off the machine, clearing my throat to mask my excitement. "Hey, I'm here."

"Where have you been?" Rachel's voice was a blend of relief and frustration. "I've been trying to reach you for over two weeks. Didn't Eddie pass along any of my messages?"

I glanced over at Eddie, sprawled on the couch with his feet dangling off one armrest and his head lolling upside down off a cushion. A thin line of drool connected his slack mouth to the floor. Amid the sea of beer cans on the coffee table, I noticed three unfamiliar faces passed out on the floor. The scene painted a grim picture of what had become our daily reality.

I slapped my hand across Eddie's forehead, more out of frustration than an attempt to wake him. "No, Eddie DIDN'T give me any of your messages, RACHEL!" I said loudly, emphasizing her name. Eddie stirred just long enough to mumble an obscenity before slipping back into his alcohol-induced slumber.

Rachel sighed, a sound laden with unspoken words. "Well, anyway... I wanted to let you know what time you can pick me up this Saturday."

My insides plummeted. This was the moment I'd been simultaneously dreading and hoping for. "Um, yeah. About that... Havok needs me for his party. It's on the same night."

The silence on the other end of the line was deafening. When Rachel finally spoke, her voice was a mix of shock and hurt. "You've GOT to be kidding me, right? This is a JOKE, right? Come on, Aaron. Please tell me you're joking."

I began to second-guess my decision, Havok's words about his relationship with Rachel echoing in my mind. But then I remembered how, until I started working at the station, Rachel had never shown any interest in me beyond friendship. The bitter taste of suspicion rose in my throat. "Rachel, I can't. I just can't. I'm sorry. You can find another date, right?"

"In less than a week?" Her voice cracked, desperation seeping through. "Are you serious, Aaron? You... you IDIOT!"

"Listen, maybe we can—"

Rachel cut me off, her words tumbling out in a rush. "No! I'm not even going to have this conversation. This is supposed to be one of the most important moments in a girl's life, and you're telling me that some stupid rave is more important? I can't BELIEVE you!"

"Rachel, it's more complicated than that," I pleaded, suddenly aware of how shabby my surroundings were. "Maybe you can come over and we can talk about thi—" I caught myself, looking around at the mess. "Or maybe we can meet somewhere to talk about this."

"Forget it, Aaron!" The tears in **Rachel's** voice were unmistakable now. "Just... just forget I even asked!"

def retrieve_encoded_data():

 # >> Retrieving encoded data...

FIRE IT UP

01011001 01001111 01010101 00100000 01001000 01000001
01010110 01000101 00100000 01010100 01001111 00100000 01000011
01001000 01001111 01001111 01010011 01000101 00100000 01000001
01000001 01010010 01001111 01001110

options_data = https://bit.ly/4dFNqiZ
alternate_data = https://bit.ly/4fVYCcZ

return encoded_data

 # Data retrieval successful. [Connection Terminated]

Before I could apologize, the harsh buzz of the dial tone filled my ear. I stood there, frozen, the phone still pressed to my ear, as if I could will Rachel's voice to return.

Eddie stirred on the couch, his bleary eyes struggling to focus on me. "Yo, roomie," he slurred, "Rachel called for you last night."

"Thanks," I muttered, the irony of his belated message not lost on me.

As I set the phone down, the feeling of what had just happened settled over me like a heavy blanket. I'd pushed away the one person who might have seen past the mess I'd become, all for the promise of belonging to a world that, deep down, I knew was just as hollow as the empty beer cans littering the floor.

I sank down onto the floor, my back against the wall, and closed my eyes. In the darkness behind my eyelids, I saw Rachel's face – not the hurt and angry Rachel from our phone call, but the Rachel I'd first fallen for. The girl with the kind smile and eyes that seemed to see right through me.

What had happened to us? When did everything become so complicated?

As I sat there, lost in thought, a realization began to dawn on me. Rachel's insistence on reaching me, her desperation to secure me as her prom date – it wasn't about using me or my newfound status. It was about us, about what we could have been.

Maybe she had hung out with Havok one night, caught up in the allure of the rave scene. But something had changed. She'd been trying to reach me for weeks, probably wanting to explain, to make things right.

And what had I done? I'd chosen a party – Havok's party, of all things – over her.

The irony of the situation.. Here I was, chasing after acceptance and belonging in the rave scene, when the one person who had truly accepted me for who I was had been reaching out all along.

I glanced at Eddie, still passed out on the couch, and then at the phone. It wasn't too late. I could call Rachel back, explain everything, beg for forgiveness if I had to.

But as I reached for the phone, doubt crept in. What if she didn't want to hear from me? What if I'd already ruined everything?

My hand hovered over the receiver, trembling slightly. In that moment, I realized I was standing at a crossroads. The path I chose now would define not just my relationship with Rachel, but the person I was becoming.

With a deep sigh, I let my hand fall away from the phone. The allure of Havok's party, the promise of belonging to something bigger than myself, still pulled at me. Rachel's words echoed in my mind, but they were drowned out by the phantom beats of the rave, the siren call of a world where I thought I could reinvent myself.

I stood up, casting one last glance at the silent phone. "I'm sorry, Rachel," I whispered to the empty room. But even as the words left my lips, I wasn't sure if I was apologizing for choosing the rave over her, or for not being brave enough to fight for what we could have had.

Approaching the window, I pondered my decision under the fading afternoon light. But the die was cast. I had chosen my path, for better or worse.

The rave awaited, with all its promises and perils. And somewhere out there, Rachel was moving on without me. I only hoped that someday, somehow, I'd get the chance to make things right. But for now, the beat of the underground called, and I was powerless to resist its pull.

** **Footnote:** 0:32-0:53

Chapter 14:

"Atom Bomb" by Fluke

[110 BPM]

The air was buzzing as the time for Ritual drew near. My midnight to 8:00 AM shift at The X had just ended, leaving me with enough time to catch some sleep before the big event. Johnny had even given me Sunday off - a rare show of trust that both thrilled and terrified me.

As I sat in the dimly lit booth during my overnight shift, the weight of what we were about to do pressed down on me. The glow of the request line blinked incessantly, a constant reminder of the growing gossip around Ritual.

"You're listening to The X, Spokane's only alternative," I purred into the mic, my voice stirring with nerves. "Coming up, we've got a pair of tickets to the event everyone's talking about. Stay tuned, night owls." **

The phone lines exploded. It seemed like every insomniac and night shifter in Spokane wanted a piece of this underground party. As I fielded calls, I felt the guilt. Johnny had started to trust me with the overnight shift, leaving me unsupervised more often than not. And here I was, using that trust to promote an event that walked a fine line between edgy and illegal.

Between tracks, a familiar voice broke through the static. "Hey, Aaron. It's Nexus."

---

1. https://open.spotify.com/track/3ajbqS54UTMweMp1x24DFN?si=188479eb3df84aaa

My heart train wrecked a beat. "Nexus! Man, it's good to hear from you. What's keeping you up at this ungodly hour?"

There was a pause, heavy with unspoken tension. "This Ritual thing... it's got people talking. Saturdays are usually our busiest nights at The OZ. I'm worried, kid."

I swallowed hard, suddenly feeling like a traitor. "Listen, Nexus, can we take this off air? I've got a song queued up."

As the opening chords of an Alice in Chains track filled the airwaves, I switched to the private line. "I'm sorry, man. I should've talked to you about this sooner. It's just... everything's been happening so fast."

Nexus's sigh cracked through the receiver. "I get it, Aaron. You're chasing something big here. Just... be careful, alright? This scene, it can chew you up and spit you out if you're not prepared."

His words took me back. "I miss hanging out at The OZ, learning from you. Do you think... maybe I could still be your apprentice? Come by some Friday, watch you do your thing?"

Warmth returned to Nexus's voice. "Yeah, kid. I'd like that. How about we meet on Wednesday? We can grab a coffee, talk about what you're getting yourself into."

Nexus's words were a lifeline, a reminder of the simpler times before Havok and Ritual came into my life.

The rest of the shift flew by in a blur of request calls and thinly veiled promotions for Ritual. As the sun began to peek over the Spokane skyline, I found myself both exhausted and wired, my mind racing with possibilities and fears.

Hours later, I stood outside the Alpine-hall, its imposing Swiss angular roofs contrasted by the glitter and neon that awaited inside. The busted door handle and crowbar marks sent a shiver down my spine. How had Havok managed to secure this place?

Inside, the transformation was nothing short of miraculous. Camouflage netting draped from the soaring ceilings, glitter and metallic stars scattered across the dance floor like a galaxy waiting to explode into life. The wall of speakers stood silent, holding the promise of earth-shaking beats to come.

"Dookster! About time you showed up!" Havok's voice boomed across the cavernous space. He looked every inch the rave king, decked out in baggy jeans and a glitter-covered visor. "Listen, man, I'm sorry I've been MIA. Been traveling to Seattle, getting all this together, you know?"

With a nod, I attempted to dispel the lingering sensation of being an outsider in an event that I had played a crucial role in shaping. "Yeah, no worries. It's just... Havok, how did you even get this place? Are we sure it's safe?"

Havok's eyes narrowed for a split second before his trademark grin returned. "Relax, bro. Everything's handled. Now, do me a solid and grab some smokes from the convenience store. DJ Donald Glaude's about to kick things off, and you don't want to miss it."

The 'DON'T WALK' sign screamed at me. A limo rolled by, windows black. My heart jumped. Rachel? Dressed for prom, moving on without me?

But it was the slow-moving police cruiser that followed that truly sent my heart into overdrive. The officer's gaze seemed to linger on me, then on our three-story event space behind. As the car changed direction, heading towards our venue, a cold sweat broke out across my skin.

As I stood there, I felt torn between excitement for the party and fear of the dangers around us. I realized Ritual wasn't just another party - it was a huge turning point. We were diving into a world I didn't really get. Not knowing where Rachel was made everything feel even crazier. As the music started pumping from the warehouse, I knew it was too late to back out now.

** **Footnote:** Tune in

Chapter 15:

"Flaming June - Remix" by BT, Paul Van Dyk

[140 BPM]

As I pushed through the crowd at the entrance, my heart began to sync in harmony with the trance beats emanating from within. The scent of old wood, the echo of footsteps on the dance floor, and the flickering of the disco ball spun with suspense.

Ritual had begun, and the energy was electric.

While I scanned the sea of faces, I couldn't help but feel both pride and fear. We'd pulled it off, but for how long?

Inside, the historic cathedral-like space was a contradiction – lavish yet thrown together, a glittering facade masking our last-minute preparations. Intelligent lighting cut through the haze, transforming the abandoned space into a technicolor dreamscape.

I made my way to the elevated stage, where Eddie stood hunched over a police scanner, its crackle barely audible over the music.

"Status report?" I shouted, leaning in close.

Eddie's eyes were hollow, completely dilated. "We're g-good for now," he stuttered, his tweaker talk more pronounced under stress. "C-cops are busy. M-meth bust on the n-north side."

Eddie loomed over the crowd, his lanky frame a contrast to the writhing mass of ravers below. His eyes, wide and alert despite the late hour, darted from face to face with an intensity that belied his usual stutter. As Havok's head of security, Eddie was in his element here, his nervous energy channeled into a keen awareness of his surroundings.

"N-no drugs allowed," he muttered, more to himself than the wide-eyed kid in front of him. His large hands deftly patted down the raver, finding a small baggie tucked into a sock. Eddie pocketed it with practiced ease, his face betraying no emotion.

As I pushed my way onto the dance floor, I marveled at the crowd. Nearly a thousand people were already here, with more streaming in by the minute. The voicemail system had worked better than we'd hoped, proving that the allure of the forbidden was stronger than any fear of getting caught.

The music shifted, Havok's signature air raid siren cutting through the mix. The crowd surged forward, and that's when I saw her.

Rachel.

She stood out like a beacon in the chaos, her elegant red gown a stark contrast to the day-glo and baggy jeans surrounding her. Our eyes locked, and the world seemed to slow down.

I watched as she made her way around the edge of the dance floor, leaving her bewildered prom date in her wake. My heart raced as she approached, anger and attraction swirling in her eyes.

"You're here?" I managed to say as she reached me.

"Shut up," Rachel snapped, grabbing my hands and pulling me close. "Just shut up, Aaron. I bought these shoes to dance with you, not him."

As we moved to the center of the wooden floor, I was unable to resist inquiring, "How did you find out about the party?"

Rachel smirked, pulling a crumpled flyer from her clutch. "Oh, you know.. online message boards, just like everyone else. Plus, the limo had a cell phone."

def access_files():

 # >> Accessing secure files...

ILLICIT SITE TARGETING

01001001 01000110 00100000 01001111 01001110 01001100
01011001 00100000 01010100 01001000 01001001 01001110 01000111
01010011 00100000 01010111 01000101 01010010 01000101 00100000
01000100 01001001 01000110 01000110 01000101 01010010 01000101
01001110 01010100 00101110 00100000 01001001 00100000 01000001

01001101 00100000 01010011 01001111 01010010 01010010 01011001
00101110

augmented_link = https://maps.app.goo.gl/XJh7GfRCMHViHuR99
    research_link = https://bit.ly/3MJ9XQp
    file_link = https://bit.ly/4dClDjq
    return file_link
    # > **Files secured. [Transmission Concluded]**

I chuckled, impressed by her resourcefulness. "Clever girl."

We moved together on the dance floor, the pulsing beat masking the tension between us. Rachel's eyes darted around, never quite meeting mine. I could feel the heat of her body, so close yet somehow distant.

"What about your date?" I asked, my voice barely audible over the music.

Rachel glanced over her shoulder, a flicker of guilt crossing her face. "He'll manage," she said, her tone unconvincing.

I nodded, swallowing hard. "And... Havok?"

The name hung in the air between us. Rachel stiffened slightly, her rhythm faltering. She opened her mouth to speak, but no words came out. Instead, she pressed closer, burying her face in my chest.

I felt her trembling, though whether from emotion or the intensity of the music, I couldn't tell. My hand hovered uncertainly over her back, caught between the urge to comfort and the fear of crossing an invisible line.

The crowd surged around us, oblivious to our private drama. In that moment, surrounded by chaos and noise, we were trapped in a bubble of unspoken words and conflicting desires. The music swelled, drowning out any chance for further conversation, leaving us to communicate through the language of touch and movement – a dialogue as confusing as it was electrifying.

Then, without warning, Rachel's lips were on mine. The kiss was urgent, almost desperate, as if she was trying to pour all her conflicted emotions into this one moment.

When we finally broke apart, both breathless, I could see the conflict in her eyes – anger warring with desire, hurt battling forgiveness.

"Aaron," she whispered, her voice barely audible over the music. "We need to talk. But not here."

Before I could respond, she was tugging me towards the stage. We slipped behind the curtains, narrowly avoiding Havok's notice as he basked in the adoration of the crowd.

"Come on," I said, leading her to the ladder that led to the light trusses. "I want to show you something."

As we climbed, I could feel the heat of her gaze on my back. When we reached the top, Rachel gasped at the view below.

"Oh my... look at how many people are down there!" she exclaimed. "This is amazing!"

I knelt behind her, my arms encircling her waist as we took in the scene. The dance floor was a living, breathing entity, pulsing with energy and light. From our vantage point, we could see Rachel's date, still looking comically lost and out of place in his tuxedo.

Rachel sighed, a mix of amusement and pity in her voice. "Poor guy. I feel kind of bad for him."

I nodded, trying to suppress a grin. "Yeah, he looks like a penguin at a rave."

We watched as he wandered aimlessly for a few more minutes before finally giving up and heading for the exit. Rachel chuckled softly. "Well, there he goes. Off to find his own adventure, I guess."

Sitting high above the booth in our own private perch, we observed every move Havok made over the vinyl record playing out of the speakers. "'It's all just patterns,' Rachel said, leaning into Aaron's shoulder to look at the complex web of beats Havok was physically mapping out. 'Like code, you know? Each element interacts with the others to create something greater than the sum of its parts.'

Aaron turned to her, his eyes lighting up with understanding. 'Exactly! It's like... like the music is alive, evolving as you play with it.'

Rachel nodded, a thrill running through her. This was why she was drawn to Aaron – he got it. The beauty of systems, the poetry in patterns. Whether it was lines of code or musical notes, they both saw the magic in the underlying structure of things.

"Well, now how are you getting home?" I asked, suddenly aware of the intimacy of our position.

Rachel turned to face me, a mischievous glint in her eye. "I have no plans on going home tonight," she purred.

As her fingers danced towards my lap, a flicker of hope ignited within me, momentarily painting a vivid picture of my deepest desires coming to life. But instead, she dipped into my pocket, fishing out my keys.

"I'll meet you at Eddie's house," she said with a sly smile.

I hesitated. "I'm not sure you want to go there. I can't guarantee that you'll be...safe." Rachel had not ever been allowed to visit Eddie's trailer court growing up, her parents never allowed her to visit "that side of the tracks".

Rachel laughed, already making her way down the ladder. "I'll take my chances," she called over her shoulder. "I'll also take your truck. See you there."

As I watched her disappear into the crowd, I felt exhilaration and nervousness. Rachel was clearly in control, and I was more than happy to follow her lead.

Chapter 16:

"Keep Ya Head Up" by 2Pac

[86 BPM]

The mid-afternoon sunlight filtered through the grimy windows of Eddie's trailer, casting long shadows across the cluttered living room. I groaned, my neck and back protesting as I peeled myself off the hard floor. The warmth of Rachel's body, now absent, remained like a ghost on my skin.

I blinked, squinting at the wall clock. 2:30 PM. Christ, had we really slept that long? The events of last night – Ritual, Rachel showing up, our dance – seemed like a fever dream.

Hauling my aching body onto the sagging couch, I spotted a scrap of paper on the coffee table. Rachel's handwriting, neat but hurried: "Aaron, I will call you. - Rachel."

My stomach twisted. No "thank you," no "last night was special." Just... nothing. The curt tone of the note seemed like a slap in the face after the intimacy we'd shared. Was she regretting it already?

"Don't jump to conclusions," I muttered, massaging my temples. "You're good at that, remember?"

The silence of the trailer pressed in on me, broken only by the distant hum of traffic and the occasional bark of a neighborhood dog. I needed a distraction, something to keep my mind from spinning worst-case scenarios about Rachel.

As I fumbled for the TV remote, the screen door banged open. Eddie stumbled in, Nokia pressed to his ear, looking even more haggard than usual.

"No way!" he shouted, his stutter noticeably absent. He flicked a half-smoked cigarette onto the dead grass outside. "Ah, snap!"

I watched as he darted out to stomp on the smoldering butt, nearly face-planting in the process. When he returned, his eyes were wide, pupils pinpricks in a sea of bloodshot white.

"Listen!" Eddie hissed into the phone. "It ain't gonna be for too much longer... but yes... yeah... right... Yeah... whatever. Bye."

The tension in his voice set my nerves on edge. "What was that all about?" I asked, trying to keep my tone casual. "You got another smoke?"

Eddie's laugh was hollow as he dug through his pockets. "They're spent, man. We gotta go get some more."

He flopped down next to me, throwing an arm around my shoulders. The gesture felt too forced. "What's up with all this affection?" I asked, eyeing him suspiciously.

I sifted through the ashtray, triumphantly plucking out a sad little cigarette butt. Eddie offered his lighter, the flame dancing dangerously close to my eyebrows. I snatched it away, flicking it uselessly. Spark, spark, nothing.

"So who was that on the phone?" I pressed, growing frustrated with both the lighter and Eddie's evasiveness.

"Dude, bro, buddy," Eddie said, his voice taking on that manic edge I'd come to associate with his deepening addiction. "You gotta move out. I'm sorry. HomeOwners Association keeps drivin' by and sees your truck parked outside and thinks I got me a roomie."

The words hit me like a bucket of ice water. "Well, you do, don't you? I am your roomie, right? Didn't you tell him you got a roommate?"

Eddie wouldn't meet my eyes. "Not exactly. I told him I had guests that come over a lot. But if your name's not on the lease, you can't stay here longer than three days. Sorry, man. It's his rule. I told him you'd be out by next week."

I stood up, my body protesting every movement. "I'm gonna go get us a pack," I mumbled, fumbling with my shoes.

"What? Hey, hold up!" Eddie called. "Ain't we gonna talk about this?"

I paused at the door, turning to face him. The afternoon light caught the hollows of his cheeks, the dark circles under his eyes. When had he gotten so thin? "There really isn't all that much to talk about, is there, Ed?"

Eddie spread his arms wide, a plea in his bloodshot eyes. "You aren't mad, are you?"

Looking at him, I felt a complicated mix of emotions – anger, yes, but also pity and a deep, aching sadness. This was my best friend, the guy who'd stood by me through the whole junior high debacle. And now... now he was slipping away, consumed by something I couldn't fight.

I crossed the room and put an arm around his bony shoulders. "Ed, thank you," I said softly. "You did me a favor big time. I owe you."

"Yeah, but what are you gonna do?" Eddie asked, his voice small.

I sighed, running a hand through my hair. "I'll manage. Don't worry. I've got some money saved up. I'll start looking for a furnished apartment. I have a paycheck waiting for me at the station right now. It's enough for a first month's rent and that's about it. I'll have to skimp by for a bit, but I'll manage."

As I headed for the door, I felt a weight lifting off my shoulders. I'd been feeling it for weeks – the growing unease with Eddie's lifestyle, the parade of sketchy characters at all hours, the constant fear of getting caught up in something I couldn't handle.

"I'm out," I called over my shoulder. "Off to the station and to buy a pack of smokes. I'll get you one too, 'k?"

Eddie's thumbs-up was half hearted at best.

Outside, I took a deep breath of the crisp autumn air. The street was quiet, leaves skittering across the cracked pavement. I thought about Rachel, about the rave, about the music that seemed to pulse in my veins now. There was a whole world out there, beyond this rundown neighborhood and Eddie's spiral.

As I climbed into my Dodge, I caught a glimpse of myself in the rearview mirror. The guy staring back at me looked different – older, maybe a little wiser. I thought about Nexus's words about the power of music, about finding your true path.

"Time to move on," I murmured, starting the engine. "Though I don't know exactly where."

The radio crackled to life, a familiar beat filling the cab. I smiled, despite everything. Whatever came next, I knew one thing for certain – the music would guide me.

Chapter 17:

"Rearviewmirror" by Pearl Jam

[79 BPM]

I chugged into the KXXS parking lot, my truck running on fumes and my body running on even less. The events of the past 24 hours swirled in my mind like a hazy, bass-thumping dream. Rachel's warmth, Ritual's pulsating soundtrack on repeat, and then... nothing. Just the cold absence when I woke up alone.

Her note still burned in my pocket: "Aaron, I will call you. - Rachel."

Now, as the midday sun beat down on my throbbing head, I had one mission: get my paycheck, grab some smokes, and find a new place to crash. Simple, right?

The station stood quiet, a Sunday sanctuary. I ducked under windows, praying for a clean getaway. My mailbox yielded two things: the precious paycheck and a yellow post-it. "Call Randy," it read, with a number I didn't recognize. Another debt to dodge.

Just as I thought I was home free, the elevator dinged. Johnny stepped out, his face a thundercloud.

"Dook," he growled, "my office. Now."

The walk to Johnny's office resembled a journey through purgatory. Gold records and celebrity photos mocked me from the walls, reminders of a success that now seemed galaxies away.

Johnny perched on his desk, looming over me. "Sit," he commanded.

I sank into the chair, my body protesting every movement. "Johnny, if this is about Star Search -"

"Shut it," he snapped. "You have no idea what you've stirred up, do you?"

He paced behind his desk, each step echoing like a judge's gavel. "The Easter Bunny disaster. Butchering the Star Search. And now I hear you've been using my airwaves to promote your ILLEGAL raves?"

My mouth went dry. "It's not like that-"

"It's exactly like that!" Johnny roared, clenching his fist. "This isn't some game, Dookie. It's a business. Those paychecks you're so eager to cash? They come from advertisers who don't want to be associated with some half-baked DJ pushing underground parties!"

He snatched the check from my hands. "Maybe this'll cover some of the damage you've done to our reputation."

"Johnny, please," I begged, my voice cracking. "I need that money. You don't understand-"

"No, YOU don't understand!" He leaned in close, his words razor-sharp. "This isn't about the music or your pathetic grab at fame. It's about responsibility. Something you clearly know nothing about."

I felt the tears welling up, hot and shameful. Each word peeled away another layer of the facade I'd built.

"You don't have what it takes, Dookie," Johnny said, his voice softening to something almost like pity. "You're too soft. This business... it'll destroy you before you even know what hit you."

The silence stretched between us, heavy with unspoken disappointment.

Finally, Johnny sighed. "Take the check," he said, tossing it onto the desk. "Make it last. Because I don't know where your next one's coming from. Not from us, that's for damn sure."

I stumbled out, the hallway blurring through unshed tears. Outside, I leaned against my truck, desperately lighting a cigarette with shaking hands.

I had to call Rachel. I needed to hear her voice, to anchor myself in something real.

The phone rang. "Hello?" A familiar voice, but not one I craved.

"Beautiful!" I said, forcing cheer into my voice.

"Who is this?"

My stomach dropped. "Um... is this Aaron?"

"Aaron, this is Rachel's mother."

What followed was a barrage of accusations and barely veiled threats. Rachel, grounded indefinitely. Their daughter spilled everything – the rave, the trailer, Rachel stumbling home in the morning looking like she'd been through war.

"How dare you?" Rachel's mother hissed. "We trusted you to be responsible, and instead you dragged our daughter to some... some drug den?"

"Ma'am, please," I pleaded, "it wasn't like that. Rachel was safe, I swear-"

"Safe?" she scoffed. "She comes home looking like she's been gang-raped, and you call that safe?"

My protests fell on deaf ears. Then, a new voice – deeper, angrier.

"Listen here, you little punk," Rachel's father growled. "You come near our daughter again, and I'll make you wish you'd never been born. Are we clear?"

"Y-yessir," I stammered.

"I said, are we clear?" he roared.

"Crystal clear, sir. I understand completely."

The line went dead.

I slumped against the wall, sliding to the ground. Eddie's house, gone. My job, over. Rachel, forbidden. The future I'd imagined crumbled like ashes.

"Could this day get any worse?" I muttered, reaching for my lighter.

Flick. Flick. Flick.

Nothing but sparks and frustration.

As I sat there, surrounded by the wreckage of my plans, a strange calm settled over me. The beat of the music that had driven me for so long still pulsed in my veins, but now it carried a different rhythm. A rhythm of change, possibility.

I looked at the crumpled check in my hand, then at the endless sky above. The day wasn't over yet. And neither was I.

Standing up, I brushed the dirt from my jeans. There was a whole world beyond Spokane and KXXS. A world where the music never stopped, where new beginnings waited around every corner.

I climbed into the truck, the engine sputtering to life. As I pulled out of the parking lot, I caught a glimpse of myself in the rearview mirror. The guy staring back at me wasn't going by childish nicknames anymore. He was someone new, someone ready to face whatever came next.

The road stretched out before me, an open invitation to whatever lay ahead. And as I drove, I could swear I heard the faintest whisper of a beat, calling me onwards to my next adventure.

Chapter 18:

"Right Here, Right Now" by Fatboy Slim

[125 BPM]

The key slid into the lock of my new apartment. As I pushed open the door, a wave of accomplishment washed over me. This was it – my own place, my sanctuary in the heart of Spokane's coolest neighborhood: Browne's Addition.

The studio was small, but as I surveyed the space, I couldn't help but grin. A bed, a love seat, a kitchenette with a stove, and best of all – free cable TV. It wasn't much, but to me, it was a palace. Far from Eddie's chaotic trailer or the suffocating expectations of my mother's house.

"I'm stylin' now," I muttered to myself, running a hand along the back of the love seat. The fabric was worn, but it felt like a possibility.

I still couldn't believe my luck in finding this place. It had all happened so fast – a "For Rent" sign in the window, a chance encounter with the landlady, and suddenly I was signing a lease. Marjorie, the white-haired hippie who owned the building, lived in the apartment below. When she found out I was a DJ in the rave scene, her eyes had lit up like it was Christmas morning.

"Oh, how exciting!" she'd exclaimed, clapping her hands together. "I used to follow the Grateful Dead, you know. Music is so important for the soul."

We'd struck a deal – reduced rent in exchange for helping her tend the sprawling garden behind the building. "I need a strong young man to help with the heavy lifting," she'd said, eyeing my arms approvingly. "And you look like you could use some fresh air and sunshine, dear."

I chuckled at the memory. Marjorie was a trip, but her enthusiasm was infectious. Plus, the thought of having fresh vegetables at my disposal was pretty appealing. Who knew? Maybe I'd even develop a green thumb.

Outside, the late afternoon sun cast long shadows across the quirky, tree-lined streets. Browne's Addition was a patchwork of history – grand old mansions subdivided into apartments, rubbing shoulders with funky coffee shops and antique stores. And just around the corner, the beacon of late-night snack runs – a 7-11.

As I unpacked my meager belongings, the walls seemed to vibrate with a faint, persistent rhythm. At first, I thought it was just the lingering echo of last weekend's rave in my ears. But as the sound grew louder, I realized it was coming from next door.

"You've got to be kidding me," I groaned, recognizing the opening riff of Van Halen's "Runnin' with The Devil."

I made my way to the shared wall and pounded my fist against it. "Hey! Keep it down, would you?"

The music only seemed to grow louder in response. Great. My new neighbor was not only a Van Halen fanatic but apparently had a vendetta against sleep and common courtesy.

Shaking my head, I returned to the task of settling in. Every few minutes, I glanced at the phone, willing it to ring. The silence was deafening after the constant chaos of Eddie's place. I needed that connection to the outside world, to Nexus, to potential employers.

As I sorted through my laundry – employing the tried-and-true sniff test to separate the wearable from the toxic – a small piece of paper fluttered to the floor. The mysterious Randy's phone number. I'd almost forgotten about that strange call, lost in the whirlwind of Ritual and its aftermath.

My hand hovered over the phone, hesitating. What if this was another dead end? Another Johnny Styles waiting to crush my dreams?

"No," I said aloud, steeling myself. "New apartment, new Aaron. Time to take some risks."

I dialed the number, my heart quickening as it rang. A woman's voice answered, professional and crisp. "Gold Star Broadcasting, KHTK-NY. How may I direct your call?"

My mind reeled. A radio station? What the hell had I stumbled into?

"Uh, yeah," I stammered, pacing the small room. "Extension 545, please. For Randy."

As I waited on hold, the music filtering through the line was achingly familiar. It sounded like that alternative station from Coeur d'Alene, the one that had been my secret addiction during late-night drives.

Finally, a click, and then – "Aaron! You finally called! What's shakin', my friend?"

The voice transported me back to that surreal night on air, the Twenty Questions that had felt like an audition for my soul. "Oh wow, hey! What's up?" I replied, slipping instinctively into my radio persona.

Randy's excitement was noticeable by phone. "We need to get together. I've got something I think you might like to check out. How soon can you make it out to Coeur d'Alene?"

I glanced at the clock, then at my reflection in the window. The face staring back at me looked different – older, more determined. "Give me an hour," I said. "I need to freshen up."

As I hung up, a wild, reckless joy surged through me. I leapt into the air, forgetting about the low ceiling. Pain exploded across my scalp as I connected with the plaster, leaving a small dent.

"There goes the security deposit," I muttered, rubbing my head. But not even that could dampen my spirits.

I threw open my closet, fishing out the well-worn polyester suit – my lucky charm, my armor against the world. As I dressed, Van Halen's "Runnin' with the Devil" blasted through the wall for the third time that morning. For once, I didn't mind. It was like a soundtrack to this moment, this precipice I was standing on.

The drive to Coeur d'Alene was a blur of anticipation and nerves. As I pulled up to the address Randy had given me, I found myself face to face not with a radio station, but with the glittering expanse of the lake.

Randy waved me over, two cups of coffee in hand.

We strolled along the pier, the late afternoon sun turning the water to liquid gold. Randy's easy manner put me at ease, so different from Johnny's gruff intimidation tactics.

"So, Aaron," Randy said, pausing to admire a pair of roller-blading beauties. "We're changing format in a week. Going head-to-head with The X."

I nearly choked on my coffee. "Seriously? How do you plan to compete with a powerhouse like that?"

Randy smiled. "With you, of course. And a little something I like to call 'artistic freedom.' I'm looking for someone to push the envelope, someone who knows the music inside and out and isn't afraid to connect with the audience."

My heart went into double time cadence. This sounded too good to be true. "When you say 'push the envelope,' you mean...?"

"I mean a night guy with personality," Randy said, his eyes lighting up. "Someone who can be more than just a talking head. You've got something special, Aaron. I've been watching you, and I think you're exactly what we need to knock Johnny Styles off his pedestal."

I stopped walking, his words sunk in. "Prime time? You're offering me a night show?"

Randy turned to face me, placing his hands on my shoulders. "I'm offering you the chance of a lifetime, partner. Complete control of your show – the music, the segments, everything. No other night jock in the industry has that freedom. This is your shot at the big leagues."

I stared at him, searching for any sign of deception. But all I saw was genuine thrill and belief – in me.

"What do you say, Aaron?" Randy asked. "Are you ready to change the face of radio in this town?"

In that moment, I saw it all spread out before me – the late nights in the booth, pushing play on music I truly enjoyed, my voice reaching out to all the lost souls of Spokane and beyond. It was everything I ever dreamed of, and more.

I placed my hands on Randy's shoulders, mirroring his stance. "Say no more, boss," I said, my voice steady and sure. "I'm your man."

As we shook hands, sealing the deal, I couldn't help but feel..something – exhilaration, yes, but also a hint of foreboding. This was my big break, my chance to prove myself. But at what cost?

The sun dipped lower on the horizon, casting long shadows across the lake. In the distance, I could almost hear the beat of another song, one that hadn't been written yet. My song. The one that would change everything.

Chapter 19:

"I Can" by NAS

[95 BPM]

Club OZ's lingering Kool-Aid and sweat aroma attested to the prior night's revelry. I sat cross-legged in the center of the dance floor, surrounded by the detritus of the previous evening - discarded flyers, crushed cups, and the occasional lost shoe. The silence was almost eerie, a sharp contrast to the energy that usually filled this space.

As I fidgeted with a torn flyer, my mind raced with possibilities. Randy's offer of artistic freedom at the radio station felt like a golden ticket, a chance to create something truly unique in Spokane's stagnant airwaves. But with that opportunity came a gnawing anxiety, a fear of the unknown that twisted in my gut.

The heavy thud of the club's back door snapped me out of my fantasy. Nexus's silhouette appeared, his presence immediately filling the empty space with a laid-back energy that was uniquely his.

"Yo!" he called out, his voice a combination of amusement and curiosity. "What's this, man? Thought we were hitting the town tonight, not having a floor meeting."

I scrambled to my feet, nearly tripping over my own shoelaces in my haste. "Nexus!! Thanks for coming. I, uh, I've got an idea I wanted to run by you."

Nexus raised an eyebrow, and smirked. "An idea, huh? This better be good, 'cause I was looking forward to some quality people-watching tonight."

I launched into my pitch, the words tumbling out in a rush of thrill and nervousness. "A mix show, on the radio. You, me, live on the air. Blending tracks, talking to listeners, creating something Spokane's never heard before."

As I outlined the details, I watched Nexus's expression shift from skepticism to intrigue. When I finished, he paced the dance floor, his fingers tapping out a rhythm on his thigh as he considered the idea.

"And you want me for this? Not your boy Havok?" he asked, his tone neutral but his eyes sharp.

I shook my head emphatically. "No way, man. You're the one for this. Your style, your energy - it's perfect for radio. Plus," I added with a nervous laugh, "you're a lot less likely to start a war with the entire listening audience in the first five minutes."

Nexus chuckled, a warm sound that seemed to chase away some of the club's lingering ghosts. "Fair point, fair point. But how about you? Have you ever mixed before, Aaron?"

I felt my face flush. "Well, I mean, I've watched you guys do it. How hard can it be, right?"

Nexus's laughter echoed off the walls. "Oh man, you've got a lot to learn. Come on, let's see what you've got."

My palms began to sweat. The club DJ booth, usually a place of mystery and allure, now felt like an intimidating maze of knobs, faders, and blinking lights. This wasn't like the radio studio I'd been in.

"Alright, first things first," Nexus said, handing me a pair of headphones. "These are your lifeline. They let you hear what's coming next, match beats, create the perfect blend."

I nodded eagerly, slipping the headphones over my ears. The comforting weight felt different now, more significant somehow.

Nexus guided me through the basics, his patience never wavering as I fumbled and stuttered through my first attempts at mixing. My fingers felt clumsy on the sliders, and I kept losing the beat, creating jarring transitions that made me wince.

"No, no, like this," Nexus said, adjusting my grip on the record for what seemed like the hundredth time. "Feel the music, don't fight it."

I nodded, my brow furrowed in concentration. I tried to match the beats, fumbling clumsily.

"You're too tense, man," Nexus observed. "Loosen up. Let the music flow through you."

I inhaled deeply, trying to relax my shoulders. The vinyl spun beneath my fingertips, and for a moment, I felt it - that perfect sync, two tracks becoming one.

"There you go!" Nexus exclaimed, clapping me on the back. "Now you're getting it."

Encouraged, I leaned in closer, my eyes fixed on the spinning records. The world narrowed to the rhythm, the interplay of beats and melodies. I was so focused on the technical aspects, on not messing up, that I didn't notice Nexus trying to get my attention.

Nexus's voice finally broke my concentration. "Look up, Aaron. Look UP!"
[1]

I blinked, confused. "What?"

"Look up," he repeated, more firmly this time. "You're so focused on the decks, you've forgotten the most important part."

I raised my head, following his gaze out to the empty dance floor. "I don't understand," I admitted.

Nexus's expression softened. "The crowd, man. It's all about the crowd. I know you've never had to think about this before, being tucked away in that radio booth. But out here, in the real world, you can have the sickest mix in the world, but if you're not connecting with your audience, you've already lost."

He gestured towards the imaginary dancers. "Watch their movements. Are they feeling the vibe? Do they need something to pick them up, or cool them down? That's the real art of DJing. Reading the room, giving the people what they need before they even know they want it."

I nodded slowly, the realization dawning on me. It wasn't just technical skill and perfect transitions. It was about connecting, creating an experience for everyone in the room.

---

1.   https://open.spotify.com/track/2NPxL1QqPrD1a7OLHjVcAP?si=87646a191f4b42e4

"That's the most valuable lesson you'll ever learn," Nexus said, his voice quiet but intense. "Look up. Always look up. You've got to take off those radio blinders, man. DJing live is a whole different game."

As the last notes of the track faded, I felt a shift inside me. This wasn't just about learning to DJ, or even the radio show. It was about seeing beyond myself, understanding the power of music to bring people together.

Nexus must have sensed the change, because he smiled, a look of pride in his eyes. "You got this, man. It's gonna take practice, and you're gonna mess up plenty more times. But that's how you learn. We're gonna make some magic, you and me."

As we packed up the equipment, the anticipation of what lay ahead buzzed between us. The mix show, the late-night radio adventures, the chance to bring something new to Spokane's airwaves. But more than that, I felt the weight of Nexus's lessons settling into my bones.

Look up. Connect. Feel the music, but never forget the people you're playing for.

As we left the club, stepping out into the fading afternoon light, I knew that whatever came next, I was ready to face it head-on. With Nexus by my side and these new lessons in my heart, the future was an open track, just waiting for us to drop the needle.

** **Footnote:** 0:56-1:16

Chapter 20:

"The Power" by SNAP!

[109 BPM]

"...Testing. Testing. Line one. You are on the air..."

The warm glow of sunset bathed the Coeur d'Alene beachfront as I settled into my familiar studio chair. Through the large windows, I could see tourists and locals strolling along the shore, some glancing curiously at the illuminated "ON AIR" sign. I took a deep breath, centering myself before going live.

"Good evening, Coeur d'Alene. This is 95.9 KHIT, and you're tuned in with..Aaron! We've got a great night of music ahead, so stick around."

I cued up the first track, a pop track from Ace of Base that perfectly captured the laid-back vibe of a summer evening by the lake. As it played, I noticed a small group gathering outside the studio window, watching with interest.

"Looks like we've got some company outside the studio tonight," I said into the mic, my tone warm but not overly excitable. "Welcome to the fish bowl, folks. Don't mind us, we're just spinning some tunes."

The phone lines began to light up, a steady pulse rather than a frenzied flare.

"Alright, we've got some requests coming in. Plus, we gotta talk. Is Halloween arriving too early this year? I might have proof that it is. Stick around, Coeur d'Alene."**[1]

As I fielded calls and played tracks, I caught sight of Norm peeking over from the adjacent AM studio. His thick glasses magnified his eyes in the dim light of his booth.

During a longer song, I waved him over. "Hey Norm, how's it going over there in AM land?"

Norm shuffled into the studio, his eyes widening as he took in the FM setup. "It's... quiet," he said, a hint of longing in his voice.

"Well, you're always welcome to hang out here during the breaks," I offered. "Maybe catch some of that FM energy."

Norm nodded eagerly, settling into a chair in the corner as I turned back to the mic.

"Alright, Coeur d'Alene, let's talk about this heat for a second. Tomorrow's looking to be another scorcher, so remember to stay hydrated and find some shade. Maybe take a dip in the lake if you can. Now, let's cool things down with some smooth R&B."

As the night progressed, the energy in the studio built gradually. Nexus arrived for his mix show, and I introduced him with genuine enthusiasm.

"We've got a treat for you tonight, listeners. Nexus is here, ready to take us on a two-hour journey through sound. No commercials, just pure music. Nexus, take it away."

For the next two hours, Nexus tore it up on the turntables. Outside, the crowd on the beach grew, drawn by the music spilling out into the night. Car stereos synced to our broadcast, creating an organic, impromptu dance party.

As the mix wound down, I felt a sense of satisfaction. We'd created something special, a soundtrack for a perfect summer night in Coeur d'Alene.

"That's it for The KHIT Hit Mix, folks. Thanks for joining us on this musical journey. We'll be back tomorrow night, same time, same place. This is Aaron, signing off. Keep it cool, Coeur d'Alene."

---

1.   https://drive.google.com/file/d/0B3IGcCVXQKbSUnFkSWQwNF8wXzA/ view?usp=sharing&resourcekey=0-dVgiqeaeqHyPOhJ7Y_Tv8g

As I powered down the equipment, I caught Norm's eye. He was still in the corner, a look of wonder on his face.

"That was... incredible," he said softly.

I nodded, understanding what he'd witnessed. "It's something else, isn't it? The way music can bring people together."

As we left the studio, the first hints of sunlight were touching the horizon. The beach was quieting down, but there was still an energy in the air, a lingering echo of the night's music.

A sense of belonging to something grander lingered, refusing to be dismissed.

The music, the connection with the listeners, even Norm's strange AM frequencies - it all seemed to be building towards something.

What that something was, I couldn't say.

**** Footnote: Tune in**

Chapter 21:

"The Rhythm of the Night" by Corona

[128 BPM]

The office memo from Randy felt like a talisman in my wallet, a tangible reminder of how far I'd come. It read:

> *"Aaron,*
> *FYI:*
> *KHIT 18-34 Females 7p-Mid-9 share,*
> *KXXS 18-34 Females 7p-Mid-10 share,*
> *Welcome to the big leagues, partner.*
> *Randy"*

Five months. That's all it had taken to climb to the second-largest night show in Spokane, nipping at the heels of KXXS (The X) in the coveted 18-34 female demographic. Thrill tempered by expectation.

Johnny, ever the competitor, had retaliated with a syndicated mix show scheduled directly against ours. Pre-mixed tracks and canned humor, a far cry from the raw energy we brought to the airwaves every night. But I knew better than to underestimate him.

Randy was a curious blend of rock and roll rebellion and corporate compliance. His leather jacket, adorned with faded band patches, hung loosely over a pressed button-down shirt – a visual representation of his conflicted

---

1. https://open.spotify.com/track/5IPJsGFKtxKDPCkT8lhEjN?si=d0251a3a07a64466

nature. Despite the lines etched into his face from years of late nights and loud music, his eyes still sparkled with a youthful enthusiasm when he talked about new tracks or upcoming concerts.

Unlike the gruff, confrontational style of Johnny Styles, Randy had a way of encouraging those around him, his voice carrying a warmth that made even the most nervous intern feel at ease. He was a man caught between two worlds – the free-spirited DJ he once was and the seasoned radio professional he'd become.

Yet somehow, he managed to navigate this divide with a charm and authenticity that set him apart in the cutthroat world of radio.

Randy's voice pulled me back to the present. "Alright, team," he began, his eyes twinkling with barely contained enthusiasm. "Let's dive in."

The conference room buzzed with energy as we cracked open celebratory beers, the charts spread before us like a roadmap to radio domination. I nursed my drink, acutely aware of being underage, but grateful for Randy's tacit inclusion.

As ideas flowed – interactive trivia, remote broadcasts, retro request hours – I felt the spark of inspiration ignite. This was more than just a job; it was a creative playground, a chance to push boundaries and connect with listeners in ways I'd only dreamed of.

As the meeting wound down, Randy held me back. "Listen," he said, his tone shifting to something more serious. "I've got a proposition for you. The Coeur D' Alene Christmas parade is coming up, and I want you to represent the station."

My stomach clenched, memories of the Star Search disaster flashing through my mind. Randy must have read my expression because he quickly added, "Just drive and wave. No tripping and falling all over D-list singers in the shopping mall this time, alright?"

I nodded, grateful for the second chance. "You can count on me, boss."

"One more thing," Randy continued, a glint of exhilaration returning to his eyes. "What do you think about the station throwing a rave?"

My heart skipped a beat. "Seriously? You want us to throw a rave?"

Randy grinned. "Why not? You have the connections, the know-how. With our resources behind it, we could make it something truly spectacular."

Ideas exploded in my mind – flyers, DJs, light shows. "Nexus could headline," I babbled, barely containing myself. "We could rent out a venue, maybe even..."

"Whoa, slow down there, hotshot," Randy laughed. "I love the enthusiasm, but let's keep it legal, alright? Proper venue, safety measures, the works. This needs to be above board."

A flicker of doubt crossed my mind. Would a "safe" rave still draw the crowd we needed? But as I looked at Randy's expectant face, I pushed the concern aside. This was my chance to bridge two worlds – the underground scene I loved and the mainstream appeal we needed.

"I'm on it, Randy," I assured him, determination setting in. "We'll make it epic, I promise."

As I left the office, my mind raced with possibilities. The mixshow with Nexus, the Christmas parade, the rave – each a step towards something bigger, a chance to leave my mark on Spokane's airwaves and beyond.

Then and there, I thought of Rachel, of Eddie, of the life I'd left behind. A wave of guilt hit me as I realized how long it had been since I'd checked in on my mom and dad. Maybe my pride kept me from calling to check in or apologize for too long, and now the opportunity has passed? Still, the thrill of what lay ahead pushed those thoughts aside.

This was my time, my chance to shine. And I was going to grab it with both hands.

Chapter 22:

"Baby Got Back" by Sir Mix-A-Lot

[128 BPM]

December cold gnawed at my skin in a Coeur d'Alene alley. My breath fogged. Nexus fidgeted next to me, staring at the mess ahead.

"Randy has got to be kidding," I muttered, my voice a mix of awe and frustration. "There's no way we'll ever get noticed next to that."

The 4H Club's float towered over us, the Christmas tree nearly touching the clouds. Behind it, the high school drill team spun and flipped. My gut twisted with jealousy.

And here we were, KHIT-FM's prized representatives, standing next to a sad Mazda minivan with hastily applied station logos. Three guys in Santa hats and a family van. It was pathetic.

As we waited for the parade to start, I spotted Randy and Johnny Styles shaking hands near the judges' stand. Their interaction seemed polite, even friendly - two competitors sharing a moment of camaraderie. But then I noticed their eyes darting in my direction, their lips moving in hushed conversation.

What were they saying about me? Was I just a pawn in some larger game between rival stations? The thought made my skin crawl, and I felt an overwhelming urge to prove myself, to show them all what I was capable of.

My eyes were drawn to Johnny's float, a gaudy display that put even the 4H Club to shame. KXXS' star shock jock stood proudly on a platform that looked like a miniature radio station, complete with a mock soundboard and giant headphones. Surrounding him were scantily clad "elves" and – was that a faded rap star from Seattle? The one-hit wonder was there in the flesh, lip-syncing to a Christmas-themed version of his famous song as fake snow rained down on the cheering crowd.

The contrast between Johnny's extravagant display and our pitiful van was like a slap in the face. I felt my resolve hardening, a desperate need to stand out growing stronger by the second.

I reached for my yellow Walkman, seeking comfort in its familiar weight. But as my fingers brushed against the worn plastic, I hesitated. No, music wouldn't save me this time. I needed something bigger, bolder.

"I can't believe this is all we have to show for our station," I griped, running a hand through my hair. "This is stupid."

Norm's head poked out of the van's window, his breath visible in the cold air. "Hey, guys, I think I see the floats ahead of us starting to move! We should get in!"

I turned to Nexus, desperation creeping into my voice. "Can you believe this? Why are we even here?"

Nexus shrugged, his usual laid-back demeanor tinged with resignation. "Randy said the new budget doesn't kick in 'till January. That would explain the lack of decorations. I just hope he's got enough to pay us for this."

As we stood there, shivering and deflated, my mind raced. Memories of past humiliations flooded back – the locker room incident at Sacajawea, the countless times I'd been overshadowed by bigger personalities. And now, here I was again, about to be eclipsed by better-funded, more impressive displays.

Something snapped inside me. I couldn't – wouldn't – let Johnny outshine me again. Not today.

"I've got to do something," I muttered, more to myself than anyone else. "We can't go down like this."

I sprinted to the back of our minivan and flung open the hatch. Inside, I found a megaphone, sunglasses and a box of station bumper stickers. A plan – reckless, outrageous, and potentially career-ending – began to form in my mind.

"Norm, get out of the van," I barked, my voice taking on an edge I barely recognized. "Nexus, come here. Make it quick!"

As I began stripping off my clothes, Nexus's eyes widened in alarm. "Aaron, what are you doing? Oh man!" He instinctively threw his arms out to cover me, but I was already down to my boxers.

The moment my clothes came off, an unnatural chill swept over me. It went beyond the winter air, seeping into my bones with an almost supernatural intensity. For a split second, I could have sworn I saw some of the spectators' eyes glowing red in the reflection of the Christmas lights, but I shook it off as a trick of the light.

With frantic energy, I began peeling stickers and plastering them all over my nearly naked body – arms, legs, chest, everywhere. "Norm, get my backside! Nexus, get my legs!"

Nexus took a step back, shaking his head. "Man, I ain't touching any of that. What's gotten into you? Are you crazy?"

Norm, bless his heart, didn't hesitate. He slapped stickers on my back and rear without complaint before hopping back into the relative warmth of the van. "It's freezing out there!" he shouted. "You're going to die!"

I grinned maniacally, the chill already seeping into my bones. "Trust me, Norm. Anything beats the sweltering heat of a bunny costume!"

Nexus looked at me, his expression a mix of concern and grudging admiration. "You do know what you're doing, right? Randy said to just drive the van and wave. That's what you told us. Remember?"

I slipped on the sunglasses, my mind made up. "That's right, Nexus. We are doing just that. You guys drive..." I raised the megaphone to my lips and bellowed, "AND I'LL DO THE WAVING! MERRY CHRISTMAS, HO HO HO!"

As we joined the parade, the reaction was immediate and intense. Children pointed and laughed, parents gasped in shock, and more than a few people whipped out cameras. I pranced down the street, my sticker-covered body glistening in the winter sun, occasionally pausing to do an exaggerated bump and grind for the crowd.

"KHIT-FM wishes you a very merry Christmas!" I shouted through the megaphone, my voice echoing off the buildings. "We're hotter than ever, folks! Can you feel the heat?"

Out of the corner of my eye, I saw Johnny Styles' jaw drop. For a moment, his carefully crafted persona slipped, revealing disbelief and – was that a hint of respect? Even the booty-loving rap star stopped mid-lyric to gawk.

As we passed the judges' stand, I gave them my most outrageous performance yet, shaking my sticker-covered behind and belting out an off-key rendition of "Jingle Bells." The crowd roared, a mix of cheers and scandalized gasps that sent a thrill through me.

As my feet danced and my body pranced, a persistent unease washed over me, whispering I wasn't hitting the right notes..

Suddenly, I locked eyes with a young child in the crowd. The innocence and pure joy in their faces hit me. For a brief moment, I faltered, questioning the path I'd chosen. Was this really the way to prove myself?

But the moment passed, and the roar of the crowd swept me back into my performance. It wasn't until we reached the end of the parade route that the magnitude of what I'd done began to sink in. As the adrenaline faded, replaced by bone-deep cold and dawning horror, I caught sight of Randy in the crowd. His face was a mask of barely contained fury.

"Oh no," I muttered, suddenly feeling very exposed in more ways than one. "What have I done?"

The next morning, I sat in Randy's office, my head bowed and hands tucked under my thighs. The silence was deafening as he thumbed through the morning edition of the Coeur d'Alene Herald.

"'Parade Prance Has Deejay In Hot Water,'" Randy read aloud, his voice dangerously calm. "A Coeur d'Alene radio deejay is in the doghouse for spreading the wrong sort of Christmas cheer in Friday's Festival of Lights parade....drawing stares and sparking complaints when he strolled down the street clad only in bumper sticker-covered boxers and a Santa cap."

I dared to glance up, catching sight of my own grinning face splashed across the front page. Despite everything, a small part of me thought I looked pretty good in that Santa cap.

Randy's voice rang through my thoughts. "The KHIT-FM microphone man stopped occasionally to do a jolly bump and grind for the sidewalk crowd, which included parents with young children."

The silence that followed was oppressive. Randy stood, moving to stare out the window. When he spoke again, his voice was softer, almost reminiscent.

"You know something? I was a lot like you when I started. Willing to do anything to get noticed. But I have to admit, I've never done the things you've done. You're out there, Aaron. You're totally out there."

I finally met his gaze, bracing myself for the ax to fall. Instead, Randy's expression softened slightly.

"I'll bet you something, because I'm a gambling man," he said. "Once this dust settles and the community moves on to bigger and better things to complain about, this might just be the most talked-about promotion this station has ever put on. Any news is good news, in my opinion."

I let out a breath I didn't know I'd been holding, but Randy wasn't finished.

"But let's get one thing straight," he continued, his voice hardening. "Pull a stunt like that without my authorization one more time, and you're fired quicker than I can say the word 'fired.' Got it?"

I nodded vigorously, relief and shame washing over me in equal measure.

"I give you a lot of freedom, Aaron. Almost too much freedom. No one else in this industry would ever dream of giving their DJs this much leeway. I have half a mind to take it all away from you."

As Randy settled back into his chair, I waited for the other shoe to drop. To my surprise, a small smile appeared on his mouth.

"But I won't," he said finally. "I'm crazy to keep you on board, but this town both loves and hates you now. That's why I'm keeping you around. Keep walking that fine line, and you'll soon have the highest-rated show in this market."

I opened my mouth to apologize, but Randy cut me off with a wave of his hand.

"Don't say you're sorry. Just get out of my office and enjoy your Christmas. But don't talk about this episode on the air Monday. Just pretend it didn't happen and move on. You've got a bigger test coming up next, and I hope you don't fail me. I've got a lot riding on this raving youth-throwing, and now, so do you."

As I stood to leave, Randy's voice stopped me one last time. "Aaron?"

I turned my hand on the doorknob.

"Do NOT fail me."

Walking out of the station, I felt a mix of emotions swirling inside me. Relief at not being fired, shame at my reckless behavior, and a nagging sense that I was walking a dangerous line between fame and infamy.

As I passed a newsstand, my nearly-naked form stared back at me from a dozen front pages. I couldn't help but wonder – was this really the path to acceptance and success I'd been seeking? Or was I just running from the ghosts of my past, still trying to prove something to the world and myself?

The cold winter air bit at my skin, a sharp reminder of my vulnerability. I pulled my coat tighter around me, vowing to think twice before stripping down again – at least in public. But deep down, a part of me thrilled at the attention, at the way I'd managed to outshine even Johnny Styles, if only for a brief while.

As I made my way home, my mind was already abuzz with ideas for my next daring endeavor. A feeling of anticipation washed over me, teetering on the precipice of potential triumph or catastrophic failure. Only time would reveal whether my path led to greatness or disaster.

Chapter 23:

"Juice (Know The Ledge)" by Erik B. & Rakim

[116 BPM]

Biggie's 'Juicy' thumped through Club OZ's booth, fighting the mess in my head. I watched Nexus work the turntables, his hands moving like they had a mind of their own.

Nexus hits a steady beat on the mixing board. "This is 96 BPM - beats per minute. It's the heartbeat of hip hop. Feel how it energizes you? That's why it works so well on the dance floor.

Nexus pulls out records with different BPM ranges. "These are your paints. A 100 BPM track feels different from a 160 BPM one. Learn to use the full spectrum to take your crowd on a journey."

"Listen," Nexus said, his voice barely audible over the music. "Feel the rhythm, Aaron. It's all about the mathematics of sound and the energy of the crowd."

I nodded, trying to focus on the intricate patterns he was weaving. But my mind wandered, distracted by the flashing lights and the writhing bodies on the dance floor beyond the booth.

Nexus caught my wandering gaze and shook his head. "You're not listening with your soul, man. Close your eyes. Let the music in."

I did as he instructed, shutting out the visual chaos. Slowly, the layers of sound began to unfold in my mind. The steady thump of the bass, the crisp snap of the snare, the shimmering hi-hats... and then, something else. A pattern I hadn't noticed before.

"You hear it now, don't you?" Nexus's voice was tinged with approval. "The 32-beat cycle. It's the skeleton of dance music, the framework everything else hangs on."

As he spoke, he began to count. At 32, right on cue, a new hi-hat pattern kicked in, adding depth and complexity to the track. My eyes flew open in amazement.

"Holy..," I breathed. "It's like... it's like a mathematical formula."

Nexus grinned, his Ray-Ban lenses catching the light. "Now you're getting it. This is the language of the dance floor, Aaron. Learn to speak it, and you can move mountains."

Over the next few weeks, I threw myself into my training with a fervor that surprised even me. Every free moment was spent in the booth, watching Nexus work his magic, absorbing every trick and technique I could.

The turntables became an extension of my body. I learned to feel the music in my bones, to anticipate the shifts and changes before they happened. The crossfader became my paintbrush.

But it wasn't just about syncing BPMs. Nexus taught me to read the crowd, to sense their energy and feed it back to them through the music.

"The vibe you create changes emotions," he'd say. "Those emotions change how people act. Play the wrong track at the wrong time, you could turn the mood sour. But nail it..." He'd grin. "You can take everyone on a journey."

Night after night, I practiced, my skills improving slowly but steadily. The trainwrecks became less frequent, the transitions smoother. I started to understand the subtle art of manipulating energy in a room.

"Breathe," Nexus would remind me when frustration threatened to take over. "The music will come. You can't force it."

One night, after a particularly grueling session, Nexus turned to me with a serious expression. "You're ready," he said simply.

My heart skipped like a record. "Ready? For what?"

"To fly solo," he replied, gesturing to the booth. "Tomorrow night, this is all yours."

———

The next evening, I stood behind the decks, my palms sweating as I surveyed the packed dance floor. This was it. My moment of truth.

As I dropped the needle on the first record, I heard Nexus's voice in my head. "Look up," he'd always said.

I raised my eyes, taking in the sea of faces before me. And then, something clicked. I could feel it – the energy, the rhythm, the pulse of the crowd. It was like a living, breathing entity, and I was its heart.

For the next four hours, I was lost in the flow. Tracks blended seamlessly, one into another, building a musical journey that had the crowd screaming for more. When I finally looked up at the end of my set, drenched in sweat and trembling with exhaustion, I saw Nexus nodding approvingly from the back of the room.

As I stepped out of the booth, the rush of what I'd just accomplished hit me. This wasn't just about playing records anymore. It was about creating experiences, about connecting with people on a level deeper than words.

I thought about Rachel, wondering what she'd think if she could see me now. Would she be proud? Impressed? Or would she see this as another step from the Aaron she once knew?

"Not bad, kid," Nexus said, clapping me on the back. "But remember, this is just the start. You've learned the language, now you need to write your own story."

As I left the club that night, the beat still flowing in my veins, I knew he was right. This was just the start of something bigger, something that would change everything. Music had shown me a new world, a new way of connecting. And I was ready to dive in headfirst, wherever it might lead me.

Little did I know, the path ahead would be far more treacherous – and rewarding – than I could have ever dreamed.

Chapter 24:

"Insomnia - Monster Mix" by Faithless

[127 BPM]

The riffs of Van Halen's "Runnin' with the Devil" pounded through the thin walls of my apartment, courtesy of my ever-present neighbor, Mullet Man. I groaned, burying my face deeper into the pillow.

Mullet Man's morning ritual had become my personal hell - a daily reminder of everything I was trying to escape. The bass rattled the window panes, each vibration setting my teeth on edge, as I imagined Mullet Man air-guitaring in his grease-stained undershirt, blissfully unaware of the torment he inflicted.

"Please, Lord! AHHHHHHHHH!!!!" I bellowed, pounding futilely on the wall.

Nexus, sprawled on my couch, rolled over with a groan. "I swear, David Lee Roth is the antiChrist," he muttered, his voice thick with sleep.

I threw my pillow at the wall in frustration, then leapt out of bed. "I can't take it anymore!"

Stomping to the bathroom, I slammed the door, then cracked it open to glare at Nexus. "Hey, if I'm awake, you're awake. Up and at 'em!"

Nexus's bloodshot eyes met mine. "Just wake me when you're out of the shower. How are we supposed to pull off this party on four hours of sleep?"

---

1. https://open.spotify.com/track/4WAQc8xXKNinvCyV7SFt8D?si=d700ee468b644da4

"We'll manage," I growled, slamming the door again for emphasis. "Get up, you lightweight!"

As the hot water cascaded over me, I tried to shake off the fog of exhaustion. Months of practicing my set, weeks of non-stop promotion – it all came down to tonight. Spokane's Largest Rave Ever. The thought sent a jolt of nervous energy through me, momentarily drowning out my fatigue.

An hour later, we arrived at the fairgrounds' flower exhibit building. The committee had only given us four hours to set up a tight squeeze for an event of this magnitude. But as I watched a stream of eager club kids filing in to help, a spark of hope ignited in my chest.

"Free admission for helpers!" I called out, grinning as more hands reached for speakers and light rigs.

The place changed like magic. From cold hall to a living, breathing thing. Dark, moody, raw. Pure underground.

The concrete floors practically begged for stomping feet, while the high-vaulted ceilings created a cathedral-like atmosphere. And that enormous catwalk suspended mid-air? Perfect for the bird's eye view seekers and exhibitionists alike.

I looked around, proud and shocked. A bouncy castle for wild dancers. Cages for the pros, ready to turn them into living art near the DJ booth. Outside, a fenced-off chill-out area promised respite and grounding, complete with tents, lawn chairs, and a massive projector setup that would make even the most jaded raver's jaw drop.

"Man, Aaron," Randy's voice cut through my daydream, tinged with genuine awe. "I've never seen anything quite like this. You pulled it off, and under budget? I'm impressed."

I couldn't help the grin that spread across my face. "Just got word from the ticket office," I said, savoring the moment. "Pre-sales covered our costs. Everything from here on out is pure profit."

Randy smiled. "Fantastic!" He watched as Nexus directed security to their posts, then turned back to me. "I'm out of here, Aaron. This is your show now."

"Leaving so soon?" I asked, a hint of disappointment creeping into my voice.

Randy chuckled, clapping me on the shoulder. "Trust me, I'd stick out like a sore thumb. I'm too old for this scene. But I'm proud of you, kid. You've come a long way."

As Randy headed for the exit, pausing only to straighten a sagging KHTT banner, I felt a strange wave of emotions wash over me. Pride, but also of something else – a nagging sense that I was straddling two worlds, never fully belonging to either.

I pushed the thought aside, focusing on the task at hand. Behind the turntables, I sorted through the pile of records Nexus had lent me, my hands trembling with a cocktail of nerves and anxiety. The flood lights dimmed, and a wave of eager ravers flooded in. This was it. My moment.

Nexus caught my eye, flashing me a thumbs-up. "It's go time," he mouthed.

I closed my eyes, and dropped the needle. The slippery scratch of vinyl filled my headphones, but the speakers remained stubbornly silent. Panic clawed at my throat as I frantically waved for Nexus's attention.

He bounded onto the stage, a knowing smirk playing on his lips. "Might help if you turned up the master volume," he said, leaning in to listen. With a deft move, he rewound the track and let loose with a wicked scratch. The bass exploded through the speakers, and suddenly, the party was alive.

"Just relax," Nexus said, squeezing my shoulder. "You've got this. And remember..."

"Look up!" I finished, managing a shaky laugh.

He grinned. "Exactly. Now rip it up, Dookster!"

———

The first few mixes were rough, the beats slipping out of sync faster than I could correct them. Nexus's warning echoed in my head – this wasn't the enclosed booth of the club. The cavernous space played tricks with the sound, bouncing it back a half-beat off.

I adapted, both headphones clamped firmly over my ears, immersing myself fully in the music. Gradually, I found my rhythm, the tracks blending more smoothly with each transition.

Whenever I caught myself getting lost in the technical aspects, I forced myself to look up, scanning the crowd. I'd see energy flagging and counter with a change-up, just as Nexus had taught me. Slowly but surely, I built the energy, coaxing the crowd higher and higher.

To my amazement, I spotted Nexus himself on the floor, moving with the music. The sight gave me a surge of confidence. If I could get him dancing, I must be doing something right.

As my set drew to a close, I realized the building was at capacity, the line outside still growing. We'd more than doubled the turnout from Ritual. The thought left me dizzy with exhilaration.

As I scanned the crowd, I marveled at how far I'd come. Just months ago, I'd been fumbling with basic transitions. Now, my fingers flew across the equipment with practiced ease, weaving complex soundscapes that had the crowd in a frenzy.

I thought back to those grueling practice sessions with Nexus, the countless hours spent hunched over turntables in empty clubs. The technical skills I'd honed were now second nature, allowing me to focus on that indescribable connection between DJ and dancers.

I stumbled outside to the chill-out area, collapsing onto a couch as the adrenaline began to ebb. DJ Dan's funky house washed over me, a soothing counterpoint to the infectious rhythms inside. I closed my eyes, not to sleep, but to savor the moment.

"There you are!" A familiar voice jolted me back to awareness. "What's the deal, man? We ain't on the VIP list?"

I turned to see Havok and Eddie attempting to scale the fence. The sight of Eddie sent a chill through me – he looked like death warmed over, his lanky frame practically drowning in an oversized shirt.

"Hold up," I called, making my way through the crowd to meet them. "What's up, Ed?"

Eddie remained silent, his eyes darting nervously. It was Havok who spoke, his words slurring slightly. "Quite the party you've got here, pal. I wonder who could've inspired something like this?"

The implication stung, but I brushed it off. "You just missed my set, guys. It was insane!"

Havok's eyes narrowed. "You're spinning now? Your mix probably sounds like shoes in a dryer." He glanced at the long line of waiting ravers. "Looks like you've gone all corporate on us. Security searches? VIP lists? This ain't a real rave! You think you're the man now, don't you? Getting all this attention, stealing my gigs."

I felt my temper rising. "You're high, Havok. I'm not letting you in to cause trouble."

Havok jabbed a finger into my chest. "You ungrateful little... If it weren't for me, you'd still be that pathetic kid from high school. I made you!"

"Is there a problem here?" Nexus's calm voice cut the tension.

Havok sneered. "This doesn't concern you, Mix Master. This is between me and the sellout."

I took a step back, forcing myself to remain calm. "It's cool, Nexus. They were just leaving."

Havok grabbed Eddie's arm, nearly dragging him away. "We could've been a great team, my dude!" he shouted over his shoulder. "Remember that when your little fantasy world comes crashing down!"

As they disappeared into the parking lot, Nexus placed a hand on my shoulder. "Forget about him," he said softly. "He's not worth it. Come on, let's get back inside. Your crowd's waiting."

I nodded, but the encounter had left a bitter taste in my mouth. As we re-entered the heart of the rave, I couldn't shake the nagging feeling that Havok's words held a kernel of truth. Had I sold out? Was I losing touch with the very scene that had given me a sense of belonging?

The rest of the night passed in a blur of beats and bodies, but the joy I'd felt earlier had dimmed. When the sun rose, I was running on fumes, mechanically overseeing the tear-down and load-out.

I watched them load the last gear. My face in a puddle looked old, worn out. Where was I headed? The rave was a hit, sure. But what was I losing?

Chapter 25:

"Sabotage" by Beastie Boys

[85 BPM]

The fairgrounds were trashed. Empty cups and broken hopes everywhere. I stumbled through, the night's weight crushing me. The beats that drove us were gone, replaced by dawn's cruel light and the gut punch that it was all over.

Randy showed up at 9:30, fresh and awake. It was like a sick joke. I could barely keep my eyes open. We were worlds apart - the pro and the rookie, divided by years and piles of garbage.

"This place looks like a tornado hit it," Randy observed, his eyes scanning the wreckage. "Well, so much for the damage deposit. How did we do, my hard-working zombie?"

I approached him with the cash drawer, trying to summon some enthusiasm. "It's all there, Boss. Count it. A thousand tickets paid for at the door, ten bucks a head. You got twenty grand. Pure profit. Not to mention two pre-sales at Ticketmaster."

As Randy opened the box and handed me my share, I searched his face for approval. There was pride there, sure, but something else too. A shadow I couldn't quite place.

"Aaron, what can I say..." he began, his voice trailing off.

"You can say, I am THE MAN!" I blurted out, desperate for validation. "That's what you can say. I'm the man. Yeah!"

The words sounded hollow even to my own ears. I slumped onto the concrete floor, resting my head in my hands. The adrenaline that had carried me through the night was fading fast, leaving behind a bone-deep exhaustion.

Randy's voice softened. "You need sleep," he said, stating the obvious. "You worked hard, Aaron. Take tomorrow and Monday off. You earned it."

As he turned to leave, he paused. "And, oh yeah...come into my office Tuesday so we can talk."

Something in his tone sent a warning, cutting through the fog of fatigue. But before I could question him, he was gone, leaving me alone in the cavernous space.

The next two days passed in a blur of fitful sleep and hazy consciousness. Even Mullet Man's usual morning concert couldn't penetrate the depths of my exhaustion.

As I fumbled with my keys one morning, the scent of motor oil exhaust and American Spirits assaulted my nostrils. Mullet Man's door stood ajar, offering an unwanted glimpse into his cluttered living room. Beer cans and car magazines littered every surface, a shrine to wasted potential.

I thought of a future version of myself, of endless weekends spent under the hood of a truck that outlived its lifespan. The memory of oil-stained fingers and broken promises rose like bile in my throat. No, I wouldn't become that. I couldn't.

When Tuesday finally arrived, I felt rejuvenated, ready to bask in the glow of our success.

But as I walked through the halls of the station, the atmosphere was all wrong. A palpable tension hung in the air, faces turned away as I passed. And then there was Randy, his usual easy-going demeanor replaced by something grimmer.

"Aaron, come into my office," he said, his voice devoid of its usual warmth.

In that silent moment, we faced each other, a tangible barrier stretching between us. "Something wrong, Boss?" I ventured, my stomach churning. "Everything all right?"

Randy's eyes met mine, and in that moment, I knew. Whatever was coming, it wasn't good.

"It's... It's all I can say is we tried. But we had no choice. We had to do it."

My mind raced, grasping for explanations. The ratings weren't due for weeks. Our night show was gaining traction. The mix show was solid. And the rave... the rave had been a triumph. Hadn't it?

"We are changing the format again," Randy finally said, the words falling like hammer blows.

I blinked, struggling to process. "Um... I... but... To what?" I stammered. "What are we...? Why? I'm lost here."

Randy's shoulders sagged. "We're going soft rock."

I clung to hope. "Well, that's not much of a stretch for me," I said, forcing a smile. "I can still be real with this format." We'll have to drop the mix show; that's gonna be a bummer. But, hey, I can adapt. Right? Yeah, I can make the transition. No problem. Is that it? Ah, no worries then. Whew! Man, for a second there I thought I was being fired."

The nervous laughter died in my throat as I noticed Randy's expression. Before he could respond, the office door swung open.

"What's he still doing here?" a familiar voice growled. "I thought you were going to call him yesterday!"

Johnny. My nemesis, my rival, the very embodiment of everything I'd been fighting against. What the heck was he doing here?

Randy's eyes met Johnny's, a silent exchange that spoke volumes. "I couldn't do something like this over the phone, Johnny," he said softly. "This needed to be done face to face."

The pieces clicked into place with sickening clarity. I stood, my body moving of its own accord. "What needed to be done face to face?" I demanded, my voice rising. "Randy? Dude! What is he talking about and why is he here?"

At long last, Randy's gaze connected with mine, carrying a blend of shame and acceptance. "Aaron, we sold the radio station. I'm sorry. I didn't want to tell you like this."

The world tilted on its axis. Johnny's smug voice roared in my ears. "Just watch the Dookster," he sneered. "The tears will start flowing any second now."

But Johnny was wrong. There were no tears, not this time. Just a white-hot rage that burned away everything else.

"So, it's like that, huh?" I spat, rounding on Randy. "I can understand where you're coming from. I don't blame you. Sell it if you have to, but sell it to our DIRECT COMPETITOR?" **

Randy's explanation washed over me, words like "upper management" and "too good to pass up" barely registering. All I could focus on was Johnny's triumphant grin, the living embodiment of everything I'd lost.

I got in his face, close enough to see the flecks of gold in his brown eyes. "You think I'm just going to shrivel up and die?" I growled. "You have not seen the last of me, Johnny. Mark my words!"

As I stormed out of the office, leaving behind the shattered remains of my dreams, a strange calm settled over me. This wasn't the end. It couldn't be. Somewhere in the wreckage of my career, there had to be a way forward.

The beats that had driven me for so long still pulsed in my veins, a reminder of the power I'd wielded, if only for a moment. And as I stepped out into the harsh light of day, I knew one thing for certain:

I wasn't done. Not by a long shot.

** **Footnote:** 0:15-0:40

Chapter 26:

"Firestarter" by The Prodigy

[142 BPM]

My bedside clock flashed 1:30 AM, its angry red numbers cutting through the gloom of my tiny flat. My sleep schedule had been thrown into chaos since our last party, leaving me wide awake while Nexus slumbered peacefully on my worn-out couch.

I envied his ability to find rest so easily. As I lay there, my mind racing with the events of the past few days, I realized sleep wouldn't come without some help. Quietly, I reached for my trusty yellow Walkman and slipped on the headphones, careful not to wake Nexus.

The nostalgic crackle of the AM band filled my ears as I tuned through the frequencies. Talk radio had become my lullaby, the droning voices a comforting white noise that drowned out the constant beats on repeat in my head. But tonight, as I settled on Art Bell's familiar timbre, something felt different.

Art's voice, usually a soothing balm to my frayed nerves, held an edge I'd never heard before. It made the hair on the back of my neck stand up.

"Ladies and gentlemen," Art said, his words measured and careful, "I've just received some disturbing information. A team of scientists in Siberia claims to have recorded... well, I can only describe it as the sounds of Hell itself."

My breath caught in my throat. The Siberian Hell Sounds - I'd heard whispers about this urban legend, but never thought I'd hear actual evidence.

"What you're about to hear," Art continued, "is allegedly a recording taken from a borehole over 14 kilometers deep. The scientists reported hearing human screams and cries of anguish before their equipment melted from the extreme heat. Listeners, I warn you - this audio is deeply disturbing. Proceed with caution."

My finger hovered over the volume dial, part of me wanting to turn it off, to retreat into the safety of silence. But I couldn't. The DJ in me, the part that lived for those moments of perfect synchronicity between sound and audience, knew I had to listen.

As the first notes of the recording filled my headphones, chills. It was unlike anything I'd ever heard - a discord of screams and wails, underscored by a deep rhythm that seemed to resonate with my very soul. The sounds were raw, primal, filled with a terror so pure it made my heart race.

I could almost see it - a vast, cavernous space, illuminated by flickering flames. Shadows writhed on the walls, taking on grotesque, inhuman shapes. The screams echoed off unseen surfaces, multiplying, building upon each other until they became a symphony of agony.

Beneath it all, that rhythm. A heartbeat from the depths of the earth, steady and relentless. It called to me, speaking to some dark, hidden part of my psyche.

Suddenly, a particularly agonized wail sliced through the chaos, so piercing and full of despair that I tore the headphones off, gasping for air. The silence of my apartment felt oppressive, unnatural after what I'd just heard.

My hands shook as I reached for my phone, dialing the station with trembling fingers.

"KTOK-AM, you're on the air," came Norm's nasally voice.

"Norm!" I hissed, trying not to wake Nexus. "It's Aaron... Tell me you're recording this."

There was a long pause, filled only with the sound of Norm's shallow breathing.

"I... I heard it," he finally whispered, his voice quavering. "Oh no, Aaron. What was that?"

"You've got to make me a copy," I said, my voice urgent. "This could change everything."

Norm agreed to mail his old radio friend a copy of the sound clip. As I hung up, I saw my reflection in the bathroom mirror. The face staring back at me was transformed - eyes wide and feverish, skin pale and clammy. I looked like a man who'd stared into the abyss... and heard it stare back.

I knew in that moment that I was standing on the precipice of something monumental. That rhythm, that raw emotion, that power - it was everything I had been searching for in my music. This was the missing piece, the key to creating something truly groundbreaking.

Nexus stirred on the couch, mumbling something about cosmic vibrations. I froze, suddenly afraid of what he might say if he knew what I'd just heard, what I was contemplating.

As I crawled back into bed, the hellish sounds echoed in my mind, intertwining with the beats and rhythms of my own creation. I closed my eyes, but sleep wouldn't come. Instead, visions of fire and brimstone danced behind my eyelids, accompanied by that relentless, infernal beat.

A new day was approaching, and with it, a journey into the unknown depths of music and the human soul. But as I lay there, heart pounding in time with that remembered rhythm, I couldn't shake the feeling that I was about to unleash something I couldn't control.

The sound from the abyss had called to me, and God help me, I was going to answer.

Chapter 27:

"Demons Theme" by LTJ Bukem

[145 BPM]

The hellish screams from that mysterious Siberian recording echoed in my mind, drowning out even the incessant Van Halen blaring through the wall. I lay in bed, staring at the alarm clock, waiting for Mullet Man's daily 6 AM assault on my sanity. My fingers dug into the sheets, knuckles white with frustration.

This was it. The breaking point.

I stumbled out of bed, nearly face-planting as I struggled to pull on my jeans. Nexus stirred on the couch, his voice thick with sleep. "Dude, what's the deal?"

"I'm ending this," I growled, snatching his van keys. "One way or another."

Mullet Man stood in the hallway, a bewildered expression on his face as I unleashed a torrent of pent-up frustration. "Do you have any idea what it's like?" I shouted, my voice cracking with emotion. "To be surrounded by... by this?" I gestured wildly at his unkempt appearance, the lingering smell of motor oil that clung to him like a second skin.

The streets of Spokane blurred as I tore through the neighborhood, narrowly missing joggers and blowing through stop signs. My laughter bordered on maniacal as I caught sight of raised middle fingers in the rearview mirror. The world had become a surreal dreamscape, reality blending with the nightmarish sounds that wouldn't leave my head.

Back at the apartment, I lugged in massive speakers from The OZ, setting them up with single-minded determination. Nexus emerged from the shower, eyes wide as he took in the scene.

"Aaron, man, you're scaring me," he said, but I barely heard him over the thrumming in my veins.

I cued up the track, my finger hovering over the crossfader. The irony wasn't lost on me – fighting Van Halen's "Runnin' with the Devil" with its own hellish rhythms. It felt fitting, given the infernal screams from Siberia still echoing in my mind.

"All right, Mullet Man," I snarled, "let's see how you like a taste of your own medicine."

The opening riff exploded through the apartment, magnified tenfold by the professional-grade speakers. The bass was so intense I could feel my teeth vibrate.

Windows rattled, picture frames danced across shelves, and I swore I could hear car alarms joining the unholy chorus outside.

"Runnin' with the devil!" I screamed along, my voice cracking with manic energy. "How's that for a wake-up call, you inconsiderate ass?"

Nexus stumbled out of the bathroom, clutching his towel. "Aaron, what the fu—"

His words were cut off as he slipped on the wet floor, landing hard. I barely registered his fall, too caught up in my sonic warfare.

As David Lee Roth's wails merged with the memory of those hellish Siberian screams, I felt a twisted sense of triumph. I was fighting fire with fire, battling the devil with his own anthem. At that moment, logic and consequences seemed irrelevant. All that mattered was winning this demented game of musical chicken.

The banging on my door finally broke through the wall of sound. I turned to see my landlady, her face a mask of fury and disbelief.

"AARON!" Marjorie shouted over the madness.

Looking at her, at Nexus's concerned face, and feeling the manic energy coursing through me, I realized that maybe I had. The line between sanity and madness had blurred, and I was dancing dangerously close to the edge.

Chapter 28:

"Higher State of Consciousness" by Josh Wink

[126 BPM]

The familiar stench of stale beer and desperation hit me as I stepped into Eddie's trailer. It had been months since I'd called this place home, but the memories came flooding back, as vivid and oppressive as the day I'd left.

I sank into the threadbare couch, my body still thrumming with energy from Ritual 2. The rave Havok and I had thrown had been a triumph, a pulsing, sweating mass of humanity moving as one to our beats. My ego was still inflated from the constant stream of praise, high-fives, and adoring looks I'd received after my set.

Now, as the first rays of sunlight crept through the grimy windows, I found myself back in this tomb of broken dreams, waiting for the after-party to begin.

Eddie sat cross-legged on the floor, his eyes darting nervously around the room. He looked worse than I remembered, skin sallow and pulled tight across his cheekbones.

"You killed it tonight, A-Aaron," he stuttered, his fingers absently picking at a scab on his neck. "R-really... really something."

I winced at the use of my real name. "Thanks, Ed. But hey, you okay? You seem a little... off."

Eddie's laugh was hollow, ending in a cough that rattled his thin frame. "I'm good, man. J-just... just maintaining, you know? Tough times, but... but we're good. We're good."

I leaned forward, really looking at my oldest friend for the first time in months. The dark circles under his eyes, the constant twitching, the way his teeth ground together even when he wasn't speaking – it all painted a picture I didn't want to see.

"Eddie," I said softly, "you know you can talk to me, right? If things are rough, I'm here. Always."

Eddie's laugh was hollow, ending in a cough that rattled his entire body. "W-worried? About m-me? That's a f-first."

The bitterness in his voice stung, but I pressed on. "Come on, Ed. You know that's not true. We've been through everything together. Remember junior high? The locker room?"

A ghost of a smile flickered across Eddie's face. "Y-yeah. You were s-such a mess back then."

"We both were," I said, settling down next to him. "But we had each other's backs. Always."

Eddie's eyes filled with tears. "I d-don't know what's happening to m-me, Aaron. Everything's so... so m-messed up."

I took a moment, steeling myself for what I needed to say. "Eddie, I think... I think maybe it's time we got you some help. Professional help."

Eddie's body tensed. "N-no way. I'm not c-crazy. I don't need—"

"It's not about being crazy," I interrupted gently. "It's about getting support. Dealing with the stuff we've been through. The scene, the drugs... It's a lot, man."

Eddie's lower lip trembled. "But what if... what if they l-lock me up? What if I c-can't get better?"

I wrapped an arm around his bony shoulders, pulling him close. "Then we'll face it together, just like we always have. But Eddie, you've gotta want it. You've got to fight."

Eddie was quiet, his breathing ragged. Then, in a voice barely above a whisper, he said, "I'm s-scared, Aaron."

"I know," I replied, my own voice thick with emotion. "I'm scared too. But you're not alone, okay? We'll figure this out. One step at a time."

Eddie nodded slowly, leaning into me. We sat there in silence, the weight of unspoken words hanging between us. I knew this was the beginning of a long, difficult journey. But as I held my broken friend, I made a silent vow to see it through, no matter what it took.

"Hey, Aaron?" Eddie said after a while.

"Yeah?"

"Thanks for n-not giving up on me."

I squeezed his shoulder, fighting back tears of my own. "Never, man. We're in this together. Always have been, always will be."

For a moment, something like recognition flickered in Eddie's eyes. But before he could respond, the trailer door burst open.

Havok sauntered in, flanked by two girls I vaguely recognized from the rave. "Ladies and gentlemen, the real party has arrived!"

"Jade! Amber!" Eddie exclaimed, his stutter momentarily forgotten as he scrambled to his feet. "You made it!"

The girls giggled, their eyes too bright, pupils too wide. Jade, a willowy blonde, draped herself across the arm of the couch. "We wouldn't miss it, Eddie. Not after Aaron's killer set."

I felt a flush of pride, quickly followed by a tsunami of exhaustion. "Thanks, but I think I'm about ready to crash."

"Crash?" Havok scoffed, cracking a beer. "The night's just getting started, Aaron. Or should I say... the Artist Formerly Known as Dookie?"

Amber, all curves and dark curls, raised an eyebrow. "Aaron? What happened to the fancy DJ name?"

I shrugged, suddenly uncomfortable. "Just... simplifying things. Going back to basics."

"Back to boring, you mean," Havok sneered. He turned to the girls, his voice dropping conspiratorially. "Our boy here thinks he's too good for nicknames now. Mr. Big Shot Radio DJ."

I felt a flare of anger, quickly tamped down by exhaustion. "It's not like that, Havok. I just... I want to be me. Just Aaron."

Jade laughed, the sound sharp and brittle. "Just Aaron? Honey, in this scene, nobody's 'just' anything."

I watched as Havok's hands found their way to Amber's shoulders, kneading roughly. She leaned into his touch, eyes fluttering closed. Something about the way he handled her made my skin crawl.

"You look tired, Aaron," Amber purred, her eyes snapping open to fix on me. "We've got something that'll wake you right up."

Before I could protest, she was reaching into her bra, producing a small vial filled with crystalline powder. My mouth went dry.

"Whoa, hold up," I started, but Havok cut me off.

"Come on, Aaron. You've been riding this scene for months now. Time to commit." His eyes were hard, challenging. "Unless you're too good for us now?"

I looked around the room – at Eddie, fidgeting and unfocused; at the girls, beautiful but hollow-eyed; at Havok, radiating a predatory energy that set my teeth on edge. This was my world now, wasn't it? The late nights, the pounding beats, the constant chase for the next high – whether from the music or something more chemical.

"Aaron," Jade whispered, leaning in close. Her breath was hot against my ear. "Don't you want to feel alive?"

I closed my eyes, images flashing behind my lids. Rachel's smile, fading into memory. The disappointment of my neglected mother and father. Nexus's warnings about the dark side of the scene. And underneath it all, the steady, seductive thrum of the beat that had become my lifeline.

When I opened my eyes, my decision was made. "Alright," I heard myself say, as if from a great distance. "Show me what you've got."

As Amber began to prepare the lines, I caught a glimpse of myself in the cracked mirror on Eddie's wall. The face staring back was a stranger's – pale, drawn, eyes burning with a desperate hunger I barely recognized.

Just Aaron, I thought bitterly. This is who Aaron is now.

I leaned forward, towards the promise of oblivion, of belonging, of escape. The beat pulsed in my veins, drowning out the last whispers of doubt.

This was my world now. For better or worse.

Chapter 29:

"More Human Than Human" by White Zombie

[101 BPM]

Invincible. If there's one word that captures the essence of a meth high, that's it. Invincible...

Neon smears flew by as Havok's Jetta raced through town. My heart ran on high octane, synapses firing like a fireworks finale. We were gods, kings, untouchable.

"Yo, Aaron!" Havok's voice cut through the heavy bass, his words machine-gun rapid. "You got a needle and thread?"

I white-knuckled the door handle as we took a corner at warp speed. "The fu–? Why?"

"'Cause I'm RIPPED!" Havok howled, slamming the gas. We caught air off a speed bump, my stomach lurching. "Hang on, baby!"

He yanked the e-brake, and the world went on its axis. When it settled, we were perfectly parked between two yellow lines, inches from disaster.

"Holy mother of," I panted, prying my fingers off the handle.

Havok's manic grin split his face. "Always wanted to do that!"

NorthTown loomed before us, a concrete monolith of capitalism. My skin crawled with eagerness – or maybe that was just the meth. Hard to tell anymore.

We hit The Gap first, Havok trying to play it cool as he twitched and scratched. "We'll just leave these flyers here," he told the manager, all fake professionalism.

She eyed us over her glasses, disgust barely hidden. "Sorry. Can't."

"You can't," I snarled, knocking over her perfect stack of jeans. "We've done this a million times!"

Her eyes narrowed. "I know exactly what you're doing. Luring kids to your drug parties. It's written all over your tweaked-out faces. Get out before I call security."

Something snapped. The world went technicolor, rage bubbling up like lava.

"You don't get it!" I screamed, toppling displays as Havok dragged me back. "We're unstoppable! You can't silence us!"

I grabbed a hanger, brandishing it like a sword. "You can take our flyers, but you'll never take our FREEDOM!"

We bolted, adrenaline singing in my veins. Security was on us fast, walkie-talkies crackling.

"No, no, no," Havok panted. "What now, genius?"

My mind raced, a thousand plans forming and dissolving. "Split up. Blanket this place. Meet at the car in five."

"You're insane," Havok grinned, snatching a stack of flyers.

"Oh, yeah," I laughed. "See you on the other side!"

We scattered, a whirlwind of paper and chaos. I sprinted along the upper level, flyers raining down like confetti. Shoppers grabbed them mid-air, confusion and curiosity painting their faces.

Security closed in, but they were too slow, too old, too *normal*. We were lightning, we were fire, we were unstoppable.

I burst into the parking lot, lungs burning, victory so close I could taste it. Havok peeled in seconds later, security hot on his heels.

"Go, go, go!" I screamed, barely in the car before Havok floored it.

We merged into traffic, hearts pumping, grins wild. As we coasted to a stop at a red light, Havok turned to me, eyes blazing.

"You," he said, slapping me hard, "are getting crazier by the minute."

I laughed, the sting barely registering. "Ain't it beautiful?"

"So beautiful," Havok cackled.

As we sped into the night, the world electric and alive, one thought pulsed through my meth-addled brain:

Invincible. We were invincible...

Chapter 30:

"This Is Your Life" by The Dust Brothers, Tyler Durden

[159 BPM]

Days, perhaps even weeks, had elapsed. The darkness behind my eyelids was a blessed relief from the harsh reality of consciousness.

I had slept for what felt like an eternity, yet my body screamed for more. Every cell, every nerve ending, every fiber of my being protested against the very idea of movement.

My brain, foggy and disconnected, attempted to assert control. "Hand, move," it commanded weakly.

"Nah, don't wanna," my hand seemed to reply, remaining stubbornly still.

"Legs, stand," my brain tried again, its authority crumbling.

"Nope, we're tired," my legs responded, heavy as lead weights.

I surrendered to the overwhelming fatigue, allowing myself to sink back into oblivion. The darkness was comforting, a refuge from the storm of consequences I knew awaited me in the waking world.

"Yo, man. Rise and shine! It's six in the evening," a familiar voice pushed through the fog, accompanied by a persistent shaking. Nexus's face swam into view as I reluctantly peeled my eyes open, the harsh light of reality assaulting my senses.

"I must have dozed off," I mumbled, my voice rough and unfamiliar. "How did you get in?"

Nexus's expression was a mixture of concern and disappointment. "I let myself in. You didn't answer the phone all weekend. What's wrong with you? Your eyes, they're all..." He trailed off, his gaze piercing through me.

I turned away, burrowing deeper into the comforter. "What time is it?" I asked, desperate to change the subject.

"I just told you, man. Six."

"In the morning?"

"Aaron, it's six in the evening TUESDAY evening," Nexus's voice rose, a note of frustration creeping in. In one swift motion, he ripped the blanket away, exposing me to the harsh reality of my situation.

Cool air hit me. I felt like glass. My body hurt in new ways, a tiredness deeper than skin and muscle. My mouth was dry, my tongue feeling like sandpaper. A dull throb pulsed behind my eyes, threatening to explode into a full-blown migraine at any moment.

Nexus's hand on my shoulder forced me to face him. "What's gotten into you, Aaron?" he asked, his eyes searching mine. "There's something different about you."

I struggled weakly against his grip, eventually managing to prop myself up against the headboard. My gaze fell to my feet, dangling off the edge of the bed. They looked alien, disconnected from my body. My mind was a jumble of fragmented thoughts and hazy memories, unable to form a coherent response.

"Listen," Nexus paused, allowing the gravity of his words to permeate the atmosphere. "Hanging out with Havok is just going to get you into more trouble. He's a bad influence. I thought you already knew this. Why did you have to be an idiot and start working with him?"

His words stung, cutting through the fog in my brain. A surge of defensive anger rose within me. "I owe Havok everything," I declared, my voice stronger than I felt. "If it weren't for him, I'd be nothing." I crossed my arms, staring straight ahead, challenging Nexus to contradict me.

Nexus's eyes flashed with a mix of anger and concern. "Correction. If you keep hanging out with him, you WILL be nothing, Aaron. You have to realize that if you continue down this path, you'll get deeper. You have to trust me on this." His voice took a pleading tone. "Can't you see he's just using you? He's banking on your popularity to bring more people to his events. That's all there is to it."

He leaned in closer, his voice dropping to a near-whisper. "I've seen people like him come and go ever since I opened the club. They come in claiming to be the next big thing and soon leave because they can't cut it. They either get themselves into too much trouble with the law, the scene won't support them, or they get too strung out to make rational decisions."

I remained silent, his words hitting too close to home. Nexus continued, relentless in his concern. "He's dragging you down with him, isn't he? He's got you doing things you never thought you'd do. I'm right, aren't I?" His eyes bored into mine, searching for confirmation. "I remember that time you saw Eddie outside our event. You hadn't seen him in months. You could barely recognize him. He was too far gone by then. I know that shook you up. I could tell. I saw it in your eyes."

The mention of Eddie sent a jolt of pain through my chest. The image of my once-vibrant friend, now a shell of his former self, flashed before my eyes. Nexus's words were peeling away the layers of denial I'd carefully constructed.

Gently, Nexus nudged my chin up with his knuckle, forcing me to meet his gaze. "I can still recognize you, Aaron. It's not too late for you."

I jerked away, desperate to hide the tears that threatened to spill. Nexus's voice softened, tinged with sadness. "You know, they say when people are ashamed they tend to avoid eye contact with other people."

Something inside me snapped. "I am NOT ASHAMED!" I yelled, the volume of my own voice startling me. Adrenaline coursed through my veins, temporarily pushing aside the exhaustion and pain. Driven by an intense anger and apathy that surged through my veins, an overwhelming urge forced my shaking body to get out of bed.

"Where do you get off assuming anything?" I shouted, my words tumbling out in a rush. "You don't know Havok. You apparently don't know ME! How are you able to see into the future and predict what will and won't happen? I think I have a better idea of what my destiny is than you do." My voice rose to a fever pitch. "And what makes you think he is using me? Huh? Maybe I'm using him! Maybe I know exactly the kind of people I need to surround myself with to make me get to the next level."

Nexus's face fell, a look of hurt replacing his earlier concern. "Oh, I see. I get it now," he said quietly. "Were you just using me to get to the next level?"

His words hit me, cutting through my anger and leaving me deflated. "No! It's nothing like that with you," I stammered, suddenly desperate to make him understand. "I trust you, I really do. I don't trust Havok, but I..." I trailed off, unable to find the right words. Exhausted and overwhelmed, I sank back down onto the edge of the bed.

Nexus's head dropped, his countenance portraying a blend of disillusionment and acceptance. "You're not making sense, Aaron. Really, I'm trying to understand. This is so unlike you to blow up like this. This is not the Aaron I know." He paused, his voice barely above a whisper. "Maybe I was wrong. Maybe I never really knew you at all."

I opened my mouth, desperate to say something, anything to keep him from leaving. But the words wouldn't come. He was the only good thing left in my life, yet I couldn't find a way to tell him so.

Nexus stood, his shoulders sagging with the weight of unspoken words. "No, you listen, Aaron. I can't support you anymore. If you're going to continue to get high every weekend and raise all hell with Havok, then do it. But do it without me." His voice cracked slightly. "I'm sorry, Aaron... Goodbye."

He crossed the room, his hand on the doorknob.He hesitated, looking back at me with a mixture of sadness and regret. As he opened the door, he nearly tripped over a parcel left in the hall. With a final, resigned look, he kicked the box inside and shut the door behind him.

The quiet that fell felt oppressive. I stared at the closed door, the finality of Nexus's departure slowly sinking in. My gaze drifted to the mysterious package, its presence an ominous reminder of the choices that had led me to this moment.

As I sat there, surrounded by the wreckage of my life, a chill ran down my spine. Something told me that the hell I thought I'd been through was nothing compared to what was coming.

Hell was about to be raised, indeed. And I had a sinking feeling that I was going to be right in the middle of it.

Chapter 31:

"Satan (Industry Standard)" by Orbital

[110 BPM]

Havok's screen lit our hollow faces in the cramped room. The air stank of chemicals and fear.

"Play it again, bro!" Havok demanded, his eyes wide and feverish. "That's the creepiest thing I've ever heard."

I obliged, my fingers trembling slightly as I clicked the mouse. Once more, the haunting sounds filled the room – a loud noise of agonized screams and unholy wails, underscored by a deep, rhythmic tempo that seemed to resonate in our very bones.

"I-I'm getting g-goosebumps," Eddie stuttered, his hands shaking as he meticulously chopped up lines on the coffee table with his library card. "I've got a b-bad feeling about this."

The moment Norm's package had arrived containing Art Bell's "Sounds of Hell" recording, I knew we had stumbled upon something extraordinary. We had spent hours dissecting the audio, looping it, playing it backwards, equalizing and processing it in a desperate attempt to prove it was a hoax. But with each iteration, the sounds only became clearer, more terrifying – and more enticing.

I leaned back on the sofa, tilting my head to stem the chemical burn in my nostrils. The pain was becoming familiar now, almost comforting in its constancy.

"We should play this at a party," I mused, my mind racing with possibilities. "Can you imagine the reaction?"

Havok's eyes lit up with a manic gleam. "Halloween would be perfect. We could totally freak everyone out." He swiveled in his chair, pulling up a program on his computer. "Check this out – I've been working on something in Fruity Loops."

The track that poured from the speakers was unlike anything I'd heard before. Dark, primal rhythms collided with crushing bass lines and eerie, dissonant melodies. It was the sound of a tortured soul, of nightmares given form.

"Now, watch this," Havok grinned, his fingers flying over the keyboard. He began splicing in snippets from Art Bell's broadcast – "THE GATES OF HELL," "PARANORMAL," "SUPERNATURAL" – layering them over the hellish screams from the recording.

As the new track took shape, I felt a darkness set in. We were creating something powerful, something dangerous. My heart pounded in time with the music thumping through me.

"I'll test out the track on loudspeakers before our big night next Tuesday," Havok said with a sly grin, "just to get an initial reaction from the crowd. Should be interesting to see how they respond."

Suddenly, a sharp beeping rose over the music. Eddie fumbled for his phone, his movements jerky and uncoordinated. "H-hello?" His face fell as he listened, all color draining from his already pale cheeks. "I'll be right there."

"What is it?" I asked, a sense of dread settling in my stomach.

Eddie's eyes met mine, brimming with unshed tears. "My Grandpa... he's..."

I pulled him into a tight embrace, feeling his thin frame shake with silent sobs. "I'm sorry, Eddie. I'm so sorry. He fought hard."

As Eddie left for the hospital, a heavy silence fell over the room. Havok and I exchanged glances, the crushing moment sobering us slightly.

"What's he going to do now?" I wondered aloud. "His Grampa was his only support. Rent, car payments... how's he going to manage?"

Havok shrugged, already returning to his computer. "He's on his own now, man. That's just how it goes."

I watched as Havok continued to manipulate the hellish sounds, feeling a growing unease. We were treading into dangerous territory, playing with forces we didn't understand. But the music's siren call was too strong to resist.

As the night wore on, the lines between reality and our drug-fueled creation began to blur. The screams from the recording seemed to take on a life of their own, weaving through Havok's beats to create something both terrifying and irresistible.

In that moment, I knew we had stumbled upon something that would change everything. For better or worse, we were about to unleash a sound that would shake the foundations of the rave scene – and perhaps, of reality itself.

Little did we know, the price of this creation would be higher than we could have ever thought.

Chapter 32:

"Fade Into You" by Mazzy Star

[78 BPM]

...ring...ring...ring...ring...ring...

The incessant ringing pierced through my skull like a jackhammer. I couldn't tell if it was the phone or just the lingering echo of last night's party, where the JBL monitors had blasted my eardrums into oblivion.

Cursing the sunlight streaming through the curtains, I blindly groped for the cordless, my other hand wiping a trail of drool from my chin.

"Hmmmm?...He...Hello?" I mumbled, my voice thick with sleep and something darker.

"Aaron? Is that you?"

The familiar voice jolted me awake. I shot upright, ignoring the protest of my aching muscles. "Rachel?"

"Yes! Wow, Aaron..." Her excitement was obvious, making my heart speed up. "I can't believe I finally reached you."

"Wow," I repeated lamely, struggling to process her sudden appearance in my life. An awkward silence stretched between us, heavy with unspoken words.

Rachel broke it first. "You're a hard guy to track down, you know that? I freaked when I couldn't hear you on The X anymore, but then I caught your show on the new station. And then... nothing. The station wouldn't give me your number when I called."

"You... you listened to my show?" I asked, both pride and shame washing over me.

"Of course, silly," she said, her voice softening. "How else was I going to keep tabs on you? You were so good on the air. Sometimes..." she hesitated, "sometimes I'd pretend you were talking directly to me."

My throat tightened. "Rachel, I-"

"I miss hearing you," she cut me off, her voice barely above a whisper.

I closed my eyes, overwhelmed by the flood of emotions her words triggered. "How did you get this number?"

"It's the strangest thing," Rachel said, her tone shifting. "I saw Eddie sitting outside our old high school. He looked... God, Aaron, he looked awful. I think he'd been crying. He was mumbling something about his Grandpa. Is he okay? Are you okay?"

The mention of Eddie sent years of guilt through me. I pushed it aside, focusing on the miracle of Rachel reaching out after all this time. "I need to see you," I whispered, surprised by the raw desperation in my voice.

Three hours later, I stood outside the Elks Cafe in Browne's Addition, my heart pounding so hard I was sure everyone on the street could hear it. I'd spent an eternity getting ready, scrubbing every inch of my body as if I could wash away the person I'd become. The Drakkar Noir I'd doused myself in now seemed like overkill, but it was too late to do anything about it.

I peered through the window, catching sight of Rachel checking her watch. She was breathtaking – her hair longer, her outfit trendy and elegant. She looked like she belonged in a different world, one far removed from the grimy underbelly of the rave scene I'd immersed myself in.

As I watched, she gathered her red purse and rose from the booth, tossing a crumpled napkin onto the table. Our eyes met as she pushed open the door. I saw a flicker of something in her gaze – disappointment, maybe even fear.

"You scared me," she said, her voice tight. "I thought you were going to pull another one of your legendary no-shows."

I opened my mouth to apologize, but she continued, her words rushing out like a dam breaking. "I've been listening to you, Aaron. On radio, on your shows. I kept hoping to hear the real you, the Aaron I knew. But you're always hiding behind these personas. I don't even know who you are anymore."

Her eyes glistened with unshed tears. "Ever since you chose this... this life over what we had, I've never been the same. Do you understand that?"

I wanted to reach out, to comfort her, but something held me back. Pride, maybe. Or fear of what I might find if I let my guard down.

Rachel's voice trembled as she continued. "I used to think what you did was exciting. Glamorous, even. But now? Now I see what it's really doing to you. You're self-destructing, Aaron, and you can't even see it."

She leaned in close, her eyes searching mine. "Are you okay? Really okay?"

I am invincible, I told myself. I am invincible.

But even as I thought it, I knew it was a lie. I was crumbling, and Rachel could see right through me.

"You're right," I said, my voice hollow. "I'm not the same person I was. But I'm fine, Rachel. Really."

She shook her head, disappointment etched across her beautiful features. "No, you're not. And I can't... I can't do this anymore."

As she turned to leave, I reached for her, finally allowing my mask to slip. "Rachel, wait. Please."

Rachel paused, looking back at me with a mixture of longing and resignation. "I'm sorry, Aaron. But I must tell you something. That night, after the first rave... when I stayed with you at Eddie's..."

I held my breath, remembering that night with crystal clarity despite the haze that had settled over so much of my recent past.

"I didn't feel safe," **Rachel** admitted, her voice barely above a whisper. "That place, the people... I tried to be brave, I really did. But after what happened with Havok, I just couldn't..."

```
def initiate_extraction():
# >> Extraction mode initiated...
```

THREAT EVENT LOCALIZATION

01010111 01001000 01000101 01010010 01000101 00100000
01000100 01001001 01000100 00100000 01000101 01010110 01010010
01011001 01010100 01001000 01001110 01000111 00100000 01000111
01001111 00100000 01010111 01010010 01001111 01001110 01000111

extraction_link = https://bit.ly/4cC3tx1
opening_communication = https://chatgpt.com/g/g-Sf2nRdtPk-rachel
return extraction_link
 # Extraction complete. [Link Terminated]

The revelation hit me like a punch to the gut. "What do you mean? What happened with Havok?"

Rachel's eyes filled with tears. "That night at Club OZ, when I met him... he tried to force himself on me in his apartment. He grabbed my wrist, wouldn't let go. If someone hadn't heard next door..." She shuddered at the memory.

"Rachel," I breathed, a mix of anger and guilt washing over me. "Why didn't you tell me? I could have-"

"Could have what, Aaron?" Rachel cut me off, her voice trembling. "You idolized him. And after that, I just... I couldn't sleep. I snuck out in the middle of the night and took a taxi home. I told my parents everything the next morning."

I swallowed hard, the weight of her words crushing me. "Rachel, I... I'm so sorry. I had no idea."

"It's not just about Havok," she continued, wiping away a tear. "It's this whole scene. I don't feel safe anymore. With any of it."

Unspoken words hung between us: "With you."

I reached for her hand, desperate to bridge the gulf between us. "Rachel, please. Give me a chance to make this right. I'll change, I'll-"

She shook her head, gently pulling away. "It's not about you changing, Aaron. It's about me needing to heal. To find myself again. And I can't do that here, in this world."

As she turned to leave, I felt something inside me shatter. "I'm sorry," I whispered, the words woefully inadequate.

Rachel paused, looking back at me one last time. "I know. Goodbye, Aaron."

As I watched her walk away, the scent of her perfume lingering in the air, I realized the full depth of what I'd lost. Not just Rachel, but the trust and safety she'd once found in me. The innocence we'd both lost to this world I'd thought would set us free.

The last notes of our dance had faded away, leaving only the hollow echo of what might have been. And for the first time in years, I allowed myself to feel the full weight of my choices, my losses, my pain.

I wept, not just for Rachel, but for the innocence we'd both lost, for the trust that had been shattered, and for the love that had been poisoned by the very world I'd thought would set me free. In the air, the fragrance of Elizabeth Arden's Red Door lingered, leaving a poignant trace of a memory I had recklessly discarded.

Chapter 33:

"Spybreak!" by Propellerheads

[128 BPM]

Throbbing electronica from Moby echoed through an industrial factory basement. Positioned behind the makeshift DJ booth, my gaze swept across the gathering, a blend of pride and paranoia swirling within me.

Six months had passed in a blur of sleepless nights, frantic planning, and increasingly risky decisions. Havok and I had become the undisputed kings of Spokane's underground rave scene, throwing twenty events that drew crowds of eight hundred to a thousand kids every weekend. For a small city like Spokane, these numbers were unprecedented.

But our success had a cost. The police were cracking down hard, not just on us, but on rave culture across the nation. Reports of drug overdoses and deals gone wrong flooded the news. City officials were revoking permits left and right, citing safety concerns and public nuisance laws.

"Aaron!" Havok's voice cut through the music as he appeared at my side, his pupils dilated and jaw clenched tight. "We've got a problem, yo."

I leaned in close, the chemical tang of his sweat mixing with the musty air of our underground haven. "What now?"

"Cops busted up Techno Tuesday in Seattle last night. Fifteen overdoses, two deaths. They're saying it's connected to us."

A shiver ran through me. "That's impossible. We weren't even there."

Havok's laugh was bitter. "Thankfully, your absence from that situation was a blessing."

I scanned the crowd, suddenly aware of how young and vulnerable they all looked. Kids seeking escape, connection – just like I had been not so long ago. Responsibility was heavy on my shoulders.

"We need to be more careful," I said, running a hand through my sweat-damp hair. "Maybe scale back for a while."

Havok's eyes flashed dangerously. "Screw that. We're just getting started. Next week's party is going to be the biggest yet – my record release, remember? We can't back down now."

I hesitated, torn between caution and the intoxicating pull of ambition. The drugs coursing through my system whispered that we were invincible, that nothing could touch us down here in our underground kingdom.

"Alright," I conceded. "But we need to tighten security. No more randoms at the door. VIP list only."

Havok grinned, clapping me on the back. "That's my boy. Now, let's give these kids a night they'll never forget."

As I approached the decks, the crowd lit up. That old feeling of control washed over me, drowning out my worries. I cued up the first track, a dark, driving beat that seemed to shake the very foundations of the earth above us.

For the next few hours, I lost myself in the music, pushing the boundaries of sound and sensation. We were walking a tightrope between badass and stupid, cranking up the intensity with every song. I was vaguely aware of Havok moving through the crowd, slipping small baggies into eager hands.

As the morning approached, the party showed no signs of slowing. Sweat and despair hung heavy as everyone scrambled for their next fix. I saw Eddie, his thin frame swaying unsteadily near the speakers. Our eyes met for a moment, and I saw a flicker of something – fear? regret? – before he disappeared back into the throng.

Suddenly, a commotion near the entrance. Two of our security guys were grappling with someone – a cop who had managed to slip past our lookouts.

"Everybody out!" Havok's voice boomed through the PA system. "Party's over!"

Panic erupted as kids scrambled for the exit. I quickly ejected my CD's, shoving equipment into bags with practiced efficiency. The cop was yelling something about backup on the way, but his words were drowned out by the chaos.

Havok appeared at my side, his face flushed with adrenaline. "Time to bounce, partner. Are you good?"

I nodded, shouldering my backpack. As we made our way to the secret back exit, I felt a thrill mixed with the fear. This was what it meant to be truly underground, to exist on the fringes of society.

We emerged into the pale light of early morning, the streets of Spokane quiet and unsuspecting. Havok's eyes were wild as he turned to me.

"Next week's party," he said, his voice low and intense. "We're going all out. No more hiding. It's time to show this city what we're really capable of."

As we walked away, sirens wailing in the distance, I felt a surge of defiance. We were outlaws now, rebels with a cause. The authorities could try to shut us down, but they'd never understand the power of the music, the communion we created in those dark, sweaty basements.

We were headed for a crash. Havok's Halloween party was coming, and with it, things that would change everything. We had no clue.

Chapter 34:

"Born Slippy" by Underworld

[140 BPM]

As I scanned the crowd, I was struck by how dark and ominous the costumes were. The vibrant and cheerful Halloween costumes of yesteryears were noticeably absent.

Instead, I saw a sea of black leather, pale makeup, and disturbing masks. Hellraisers with flayed flesh prosthetics mingled with Brandon Lee Crow lookalikes, their white faces stark in the dim light.

From the dimly lit alleyway, fifty eager faces gazed at me, defying the sweltering heat inside the sewer entrance. Steam billowing out of the door's grates created large plumes each time a damp attendee exited, intensifying the atmosphere.

In Spokane, there is a network of underground tunnels beneath the city, particularly near the downtown area. These tunnels were initially constructed in the late 1800s to transport steam heat to various downtown buildings. Over time, they have served different purposes, including as speakeasies during Prohibition and as shelter for marginalized communities.

"Hold tight, everyone!" I called, trying to inject some cheerfulness into my voice. "We're at capacity right now. Just hang on until some folks come out."

A girl with glittery angel wings pushed to the front, her face showing hope and frustration. "How much longer? My friends are already down there!"

I offered her a sympathetic smile. "Wish I could tell you, sweetheart. But hey, at least we're not freezing our butts off out here, right?"

The heat crushed us, worse with all the gear we'd lugged down. Sweat soaked my shirt. I cursed Eddie for being late again. His grandpa dying hit him hard, sure, but he was becoming a liability.

"Yo, Aaron!" Havok's voice echoed from the grate below. "What's the holdup? Why are all these kids still up there?"

I knelt down, catching sight of Havok's face in the shadows as he lit a cigarette. "It's packed down there, man. We can't squeeze anyone else in!"

"No!" Havok snapped back. "There's plenty of room. And keep it down, will you? One cop drives by, and we're toast."

I gritted my teeth, frustration bubbling up. "Listen, Havok," I hissed, trying to keep my voice low. "It's like a sardine can down there. The cooling ducts haven't been on since the eighties. I'm not risking these kids' safety just to make a few extra bucks!"

Havok took a long drag of his cigarette, the ember glowing ominously in the darkness. I could see the tension in his jaw, a sure sign he was on edge. "Fine," he growled. "But answer me this: What would Eddie do in this situation?"

Before I could respond, a familiar voice piped up behind me. "I-I'll show you how I'd h-handle it. W-watch this!"

I turned to see Eddie, his eyes wild and unfocused. He darted past me, arms outstretched like some deranged bird. The crowd parted, a mix of confusion and amusement on their faces.

"Yo, what's bird-boy's deal?" someone in the crowd snickered. "Dude's tweaking hard!"

Eddie flapped his arms frantically, gesturing for everyone to get down. "Get d-down! Everyone d-down!" he stammered, his stutter more pronounced than usual.

"Yeah!" a guy in oversized pants whooped. "We're about to get down as soon as DJ Bouncer lets us in!"

"No, listen!" I shouted, a sinking feeling in my gut. "Eddie's trying to tell us something. What is it, man?"

In a flash, Eddie tackled me against the wall. We slid to the ground, his body pinning me to the concrete. "Shh," he whispered urgently, pulling a police scanner from his pocket and pressing it to my ear.

The crackling voices put me on high alert. "...32-B in progress, corner of Sprague and Riverside... ETA 30 seconds..."

"Get low!" I yelled, adrenaline surging. "Cops incoming! Everyone behind the dumpsters, now!"

The crowd scattered, diving for cover. I observed one kid frantically emptying a backpack full of mushrooms into a trash can before ducking out of sight. The wail of sirens grew louder, red and blue lights painting the alley entrance in an eerie glow.

We held our breath as the police cruiser roared past, the engine's rumble fading into the distance. Havok poked his head up through the grate, eyes wide. "What happened? Where'd they go?"

"P-prostitution sting on S-Sprague," Eddie muttered, his body still trembling against mine.

"Too close," Havok hissed. "Get everyone inside, now!"

The ravers didn't need to be told twice. They scrambled down the ladder, the grate clanging shut behind the last of them. As the pounding bass faded to a dull thrum, I turned to Eddie, my heart still thumping.

"Thanks, man," I said, clasping his shoulder. "Quick thinking with that scanner."

Eddie nodded jerkily, fumbling in his pockets. A baggie of pills slipped from his fingers, clattering to the ground. He scooped them up hastily, but not before I noticed the colorful array inside.

"Oh, Ed," I whispered, concern etching my features. "That's... a lot. Are you planning on sleeping ever again?"

His eyes met mine, hollow and haunted. "If I fall asleep," he murmured, "I m-might not want to w-wake up."

I felt those words. I wanted to say something, anything, to ease the pain I saw in my friend's face. But the moment passed, and Eddie was already heading for the grate.

"Come on," I said, pushing my worries aside for now. "I'm up soon. Keep an ear on that scanner, yeah? And... maybe hook me up with something to take the edge off?"

Eddie wordlessly pressed three pills into my palm. As we descended into the heart of our underground kingdom, I sensed impending danger. The beat called to us, promising escape and transcendence. But at what cost?

The grate clanged shut above us, sealing us into our neon-lit paradise. For better or worse, the night had begun.

Chapter 35:

"Come to Daddy - Pappy Mix" by Aphex Twin

[162 BPM]

It was hot as hell, the heat crushing down on the squirming crowd. Each burst from the Peace Patrol's super soakers evaporated instantly, offering no relief. I struggled to maintain control, both of my set and my own consciousness, as the effects of the three ecstasy pills coursed through my system.

A group of Matrix-inspired ravers caught my eye, their long black coats swirling as they danced. Nearby, a cluster of Scream masks bobbed in sync, their elongated white faces eerily blank in the flashing lights. Even the few vampire costumes I spotted seemed more Anne Rice than Bela Lugosi - all Victorian lace and brooding expressions.

I spotted Eddie across the room, his gaunt face painted like a skull. When did my best friend start to look like one of the undead? As he disappeared into the throng of writhing bodies, I couldn't help but wonder if we were all becoming ghosts of our former selves.

My mind flashed back to my first rave - the warm smiles, the sense of belonging, the purity of connection through music. How far we'd strayed from that innocence. Now, as I gazed out at the crowd, those once-welcoming faces seemed twisted, almost demonic in the nausea-inducing strobes.

Jade and Amber writhed before me, their movements serpentine and hypnotic. Their touch sent shivers through me, but beneath the pleasure lurked a growing sense of unease. The turntables before me seemed to warp and shift, and I struggled to keep the beat steady.

"You okay, DJ?" Amber's voice blurred through the haze, concern mingling with amusement.

I nodded, not trusting my voice. The paranoia was creeping in, tendrils of fear wrapping around my thoughts. I reached for the water bottle Amber offered, only to gag as vodka burned down my throat.

The next few moments were a blur of shame and panic as I stumbled and fell all over the equipment. Havok's mocking voice rang out as he took over, the air raid siren cutting through the shocked silence of the crowd.

"Get him some water and put him in the VIP room!"

The "VIP room" was nothing more than a cramped, foul-smelling bathroom. As I huddled there, trying to regain my composure, a commotion outside caught my attention. The swarm of ravers pushing towards the exits, faces contorted in fear and desperation, was unlike the joyful crowds of my early days.

Red and blue lights flickered ominously on walls near the sewer grates. With growing horror, I realized the police had arrived. Panic gripped me as I stumbled back towards the main room, desperate to warn Havok and shut down the party before disaster struck.

As I reached the stage, Havok's eyes met mine, a wicked gleam of expectancy visible even in the chaotic lighting. "Perfect timing," he mouthed, reaching for a particular record.

My blood ran cold as I recognized the label - the Siberian "Sounds of Hell" recording we'd remixed. "Havok, no!" I shouted, but my voice was lost in the thunderous bass.

As soon as the record started spinning, the vibe changed completely. Havok's beats mixed with screams from hell, twisting everything into some kind of nightmare soundtrack.

I watched in horror as the crowd's movements became frenzied, almost violent. Where once I saw smiles and ecstasy, now I saw twisted grimaces and eyes filled with something darker than mere drug-induced euphoria. It was as if we'd opened a portal to another realm, unleashing forces we couldn't comprehend or control. **

In a moment of panic-driven clarity, I lunged for the power strip, desperate to silence the unholy sound. My fingers closed around the cord just as a surge of bodies slammed into me. I yanked hard, plunging the entire room into darkness and silence.

The pitch black silence scared me more than anything that night. Screams of genuine fear pierced the air, followed by the sickening sounds of bodies falling, crushing against each other in the pitch black.

"Aaron!" Havok's voice rose through the chaos. "What did you do?"

Before I could respond, blinding beams of light pierced through the darkness. Authoritative police voices filled the air, bringing with them a new wave of panic.

As my eyes adjusted, I took in the scene before me. The once-vibrant rave had devolved into a nightmare of tangled limbs and terrified faces. We had sought to create the ultimate party experience, but in our arrogance and recklessness, we'd instead manifested our own vision of hell.

The enormity of our actions – my actions – hit me like a ton of bricks. As handcuffs closed around my wrists, I saw Eddie, pale and trembling in the corner. Our eyes met for a brief moment, and I saw in his gaze a mirror of my own fear and regret.

This was the culmination of our journey, the dark fruit of our obsession with pushing boundaries and chasing the next high. As I was escorted away, the haunting melodies of that infernal symphony resonated in my ears, signifying a profound and irreversible change in my existence.

**** Footnote:** 0:00-0:26

Chapter 36:

"Hurt" by Nine Inch Nails

[80 BPM]

Chaos hit when the cops' lights flooded in. They swarmed the place, shouting orders that bounced off the walls. Ravers scattered, a mess of neon and drug-blown eyes.

I couldn't do anything as they cuffed kids I knew. Jade and Amber, glitter and fear on their faces, vanished into a cop car. The lucky ones just had to face pissed-off parents.

When the dust settled, only a handful remained - the volunteer crew, a few stone-faced officers, and me. Havok, always the slippery snake, had managed to vanish like smoke. Some innocent ravers act, no doubt.

A burly officer with salt-and-pepper hair approached, his badge glinting under the harsh lights. His eyes were hard, assessing. This wasn't some rookie on his first bust.

"You in charge here?" he asked, voice gravelly.

I swallowed hard. "Just the DJ, officer."

He snorted. "Right. 'Just the DJ.'"

"It's just music, man," I said, trying to keep my voice steady. "Nobody's forcing anyone-"

"Save it," he cut me off. "I've heard it all before. You think you're some kind of revolutionary, bringing people together through music? Let me tell you what

I see - kids hooked on poison, throwing their lives away for a few hours of cracked-out bliss."

He gestured to the empty space around us. "Look around. This isn't about music anymore. It's about money and drugs and kids too young to know better. You're lucky nobody died tonight."

His words hit like a punch to the gut. I thought of Eddie, of how far he'd fallen. Of Rachel, and how I'd pushed her away.

"What happens now?" I asked, my bravado crumbling.

The officer's expression softened a fraction. "Now? You get this place cleared out. And you find a new line of work, because this? This ends tonight. We'll be watching."

As they padlocked the grate behind us, finality settled over me like a shroud. This chapter was over, whether I was ready or not.

I trudged to my truck, exhaustion weighing me down. As I fumbled for my keys, a muffled thump from the bed made me jump. I spun around, heart racing.

There, curled in a fetal position, was Eddie. His skin was ashen, eyes rolled back. A thin sheen of sweat coated his trembling form.

I breathed. "Eddie!"

I scrambled into the truck bed, cradling his head. He was burning up, breath coming in shallow gasps.

"Hey man, you with me?" I pleaded, panic rising. "Eddie, come on!"

Havok's car screeched to a halt beside us. "Whew, close call," he said, grinning. "What's the deal?"

I whirled on him, fury and fear colliding. "He's overdosing, you idiot! We need to get him to a hospital now!"

Havok's eyes opened wider, the gravity of the situation finally sinking in. "Nah, man. We can't take him to the ER. They'll ask questions, call the cops-"

"I don't care!" I roared, shoving him hard. "He's dying! Don't you get that?"

Havok looked genuinely shaken. Then his mask slipped back into place. "Fine, your funeral. I'm out."

Before I could stop him, he snatched my keys and peeled away, tires squealing.

"Havok!" I screamed after him. "You coward! Get back here!"

But he was gone, leaving me alone with Eddie's limp form.

Panic clawed at my throat as I assessed my options. No keys, no phone. The hospital was miles away. I glanced at Eddie, his breath growing fainter by the second.

"Hang on, buddy," I whispered, gathering him in my arms. "I've got you."

I staggered towards the road, Eddie's weight threatening to topple us both. Each step was agony, but I pushed on, driven by desperation and the fading warmth of my best friend's body.

"Someone!" I shouted into the pre-dawn stillness. "Please, help us!"

But the streets remained empty, indifferent to our plight. I stumbled, legs burning, lungs screaming for air. Eddie's pulse grew weaker, his skin taking on a bluish tinge. That's when I fumbled into his loose pockets for his Nokia to finally call for help.

"Stay with me, Ed," I panted. "Don't you dare give up. Remember when we were kids? All those stupid adventures? You can't leave me, man."

Memories flashed before me. Eddie and I were awkward pre-teens, dreaming of being cool. Cramming for tests, covering for each other's lies. The first time we snuck into a club, hearts pounding.

How had we ended up here? **

A faint siren pierced the silence, growing louder. I collapsed to my knees, still clutching Eddie. Red and blue lights painted the world in surreal strokes as an ambulance rounded the corner.

"Here!" I screamed, waving frantically. "Please, help us!"

The next few minutes were a blur. Paramedics swarmed around us, their voices urgent but calm. I watched, helpless, as they worked on Eddie. Oxygen mask, IV, defibrillator pads.

"Sir, I need you to step back," one of them said firmly, guiding me away.

I couldn't tear my eyes from Eddie's face. He looked so young, so fragile. This couldn't be happening. Not Eddie. Not my best friend.

"Come on, kid," I whispered. "Fight."

The head paramedic stepped back, his expression grim. He shook his head once, the gesture hitting me like a physical blow.

"No," I breathed. "No, no, no. Eddie!"

I lunged forward, but strong arms held me back. "I'm sorry, son," a voice said. "We need to take it from here."

The world tilted sideways, everything blurring into a cacophony of sound and color. I heard someone screaming, a raw, animal sound of grief. It took me a moment to realize it was coming from me.

They loaded Eddie in. Reality hit. This wasn't a bad trip we could shake. No more late nights. No more dreams. It was over.

I sank to the ground, my choices holding me down. The music that had once been my salvation now felt hollow, tainted. In my quest for belonging, for fame, I'd lost sight of what truly mattered.

As the ambulance pulled away, sirens silent now, I made a vow. This ends now. No more raves, no more chasing a high that could never fill the emptiness inside.

It was time to face the music - the real music. The kind that heals instead of destroys.

For Eddie. For myself. For the person I used to be, before it all went so horribly wrong.

It was time to go home. Time to make things right.

** **Footnote:** 1:37-2:22

Chapter 37:

"Return to Innocence" by Enigma

[88 BPM]

A forest green 1999 Subaru Outback pulled up to Havok's rundown apartment, its glossy paint a stark contrast to the peeling façade. The rear bumper told a story: a faded Windows 95 sticker, the emblem of DigiPen Institute of Technology, and the bold logo of 107.7 The End, Seattle's Rock Station.

As the engine quieted, the driver's door opened, revealing a figure hidden by the shadow of the roof rack loaded with audio equipment. The Outback sat there, humming with potential energy, a piece of Seattle's thriving tech and music scene invading Spokane's small-town despair.

Havok's place stank of old smokes and desperation. Dust floated in weak light through dirty windows. Everything screamed: someone left in a hurry. A figure moved silently through the room, gloved hands rifling through drawers and upending boxes.

Evidence of Havok's true identity lay scattered about - newspaper clippings of the Seattle rave tragedy, fake IDs, and a half-packed suitcase. The searcher's breath caught at the sight of a familiar object - Aaron's old truck keys, tossed carelessly on a cluttered desk.

In the corner, a computer hummed to life. Fingers flew across the keyboard, searching. There - a file labeled "HELL_FINAL.flp". The USB drive blinked as it absorbed the deadly audio, then disappeared into an Elizabeth Arden purse.

A faint whiff of familiar Red Door perfume lingered as the intruder slipped away, leaving behind only the echo.. of a door closing softly.

def send_stealth_signal():

 # >> Sending stealth signals...

01000101 01000100 01000100 01001001 01000101 00100000 01001110 01000101 01010110 01000101 01010010 00100000 01010010 01000101 01000001 01001100 01001100 01011001 00100000 01000100 01001001 01000101 01000100 00101110 00101110 00101110

[FINAL DATA SENT, MONITOR FOR FUTURE UPDATES][1]

stealth_link = https://bit.ly/3X0q3th

warning_link = https://bit.ly/3XoB2yo

1.   https://photos.app.goo.gl/VsAqQswHCRHNUXE36

2.   https://photos.app.goo.gl/VsAqQswHCRHNUXE36

3.   https://photos.app.goo.gl/VsAqQswHCRHNUXE36

4.   https://photos.app.goo.gl/VsAqQswHCRHNUXE36

5.   https://photos.app.goo.gl/VsAqQswHCRHNUXE36

return stealth_link
 # Signal undetected. [Comm Link Terminated]

Meanwhile, in Coeur D' Alene, Norm sat hunched over his ancient radio equipment, his thick glasses reflecting the glow of multiple screens. As news reports crackled through the airwaves about a disastrous rave and the mysterious "Sounds of Hell," Norm's fingers danced across dials and switches with surprising agility.

"Got you, Aaron," he muttered, a rare smile crossing his face as he captured the highest quality version of the notorious tune yet. "And now, I have the **ultimate track.**"

In the days that followed, whispers spread through Spokane like wildfire. Havok, the self-proclaimed king of the underground rave scene, had vanished without a trace. Some said he'd fled to Canada, others swore he'd gone underground in Seattle. But one thing was certain - the heat had finally become too much, especially after Eddie's tragedy.

As Havok's notoriety faded, another legend took its place. The "Sounds of Hell," that fateful track played at the last rave, became the stuff of urban myth. Stories circulated of ravers who'd been there that night, claiming they'd been possessed by otherworldly forces. Some swore that merely hearing the track could induce violent hallucinations or even death.

A single vinyl record, pressed in secret before Havok's disappearance, became the holy grail of the underground scene. Its existence was debated in hushed tones at after-parties and on obscure online forums. Some claimed it held the power to open portals to other dimensions, while others insisted it was nothing more than an elaborate hoax.

What few knew was that Aaron possessed the only physical copy of that vinyl. But somewhere out there, on an unmarked USB drive, the original digital file waited - a ticking time bomb of sonic devastation. And in Norm's cluttered basement, preserved on state-of-the-art equipment, lay the most pristine version of all - a recording so pure it could shake the foundations of reality itself.

The stage was set for a battle over the most dangerous piece of music ever created, with players both seen and unseen moving their pieces into place. And at the center of it all, unaware of the storm gathering around him, stood Aaron

- a man lost in the echoes of his past, unaware that his greatest challenge still lay ahead.

Chapter 38:

"You're Not Alone" by Olive

[134 BPM]

As Aaron sat in the booth, his fingers hovering listlessly over the controls, the request line suddenly lit up. He hesitated, almost not answering. These days, the line rarely rang - a stark reminder of radio's fading relevance in the digital age. But something made him reach for the phone.

"KHVK, you're on the air," Aaron said, his voice lacking its former enthusiasm.

"Hello?" A young boy's voice, tentative but excited, came through the line. In the background, Aaron could hear the chatter of a young mom and the faint sound of a TV cartoon.

"Hey there, buddy. What can I do for you?" Aaron found himself smiling despite his mood.

"Are you really Aaron? The DJ?" The boy's voice was filled with awe.

"That's me," Aaron replied, a hint of his old charm creeping back into his voice. "What's your name?"

"I'm Max. I'm nine," the boy said proudly. "I'm babysitting my little sisters while Mom's on the porch. I... I want to be a DJ just like you when I grow up."

Aaron felt a pang in his chest - a mixture of pride and sorrow. "That's great, Max. Being a DJ can be pretty cool. But it's not always easy."

"I know," Max said earnestly. "But the way you talk about music, how you make people feel... it's like *magic.*"

Aaron closed his eyes, memories washing over him. Highs and lows, triumphs and tragedies. "It is like magic, Max. But remember, even magic has a price."

"What do you mean?" Max asked, curiosity evident in his voice.

Aaron took a deep breath, choosing his words carefully. "Music is powerful, Max. It can lift people, bring them together. But it can also lead you down some dark paths if you're not careful. Always remember why you love it in the first place."

"I will," Max promised solemnly. "Can you play a song for me and my mom?"

"Of course, buddy. What would you like to hear?"

As Max's mom made his request for Michael Jackson, Aaron felt a warmth he hadn't experienced in years. In that second, he remembered why he'd fallen in love with radio in the first place - the connection, the ability to touch lives through the airwaves.

"This one's for you, Max," Aaron said as he cued up the track. "And for all the dreamers out there. Keep that passion alive, but always stay true to yourself. That's the real magic." **

The song faded, and Aaron held onto the warmth of that conversation. He may have lost his way, but perhaps he could still guide others on their journey.

Seven years had worn Aaron down. The kid who once owned the dance floor was dead. Now, he drifted through life, chasing a beat he couldn't hear anymore.

Despite years of speech therapy funded by his mother and the comfort of living with his father again, the wounds from his past persisted, manifested in the subtle trembling of his hands and the occasional hesitation in his speech.

"And that was... uh, s-something," Aaron's voice crackled over the airwaves, a faint slur betraying the toll of his past excesses. "You're listening to... um, KNEX? No, wait. KHVK? Ah, hell. Just s-stay tuned for more... stuff."

He yanked off his headphones, wincing at the feedback. The station manager's disapproving glare burned into his back as he shuffled out of the booth, his movements lacking the fluid grace of his DJ days.

"Aaron! My office, now!"

As Aaron walked through the hall, he reflected on his journey. He had mastered nearly every aspect of being a DJ - from club gigs to raves, from FM radio to creating groundbreaking tracks. But there was one area where he still fell short, a quiet curse he rarely admitted to anyone.

Despite his idol Art Bell's ability to talk for hours on end, Aaron had never quite mastered the art of being a talk show host. Years of substance abuse had left holes in his memory and cognition, making it impossible for him to speak at length without constant editing and retakes.

"Look, Aaron," the manager sighed, pinching the bridge of his nose. "I know you were hot back in the day. But this? This isn't working. We need someone who can string two sentences together without spacing out."

Aaron nodded mechanically, the words washing over him. His fingers tapped out a restless rhythm on his leg - a tic he'd developed years ago, a physical manifestation of the music that now eluded him.

"I'm sorry," he mumbled, not meeting the manager's eyes. "I'll do better. I just need-"

"Save it," the manager cut him off. "We both know that's not true. Clear out your locker. We're done here." The finality in his voice was nothing new. Aaron had heard it before, in a dozen different offices across a dozen different stations.

As he cleaned out his locker, Aaron couldn't help but feel a sense of bitter gratitude. In the chaos following that final, fateful rave, Havok's obsession with fame had unintentionally protected Aaron from legal consequences. Every flyer, every promotion, every whispered rumor in the scene - it all led back to Havok.

** **Footnote:** Tune In

The steps of the Masonic Temple were cool against Aaron's back as he settled into his nightly vigil. Across the street, parishioners filed into the church he'd abandoned long ago, their voices raised in joyful song. The sound made his heart ache with a longing he couldn't quite name.

He pulled out his battered yellow Walkman, the plastic scratched and faded. The headphones settled over his ears like old friends as he began his nightly ritual, scanning the airwaves for... something. Anything.

Static crackled. Fragments of songs faded in and out. Talk radio hosts droned on about politics and sports. But nothing reached him, nothing stirred the hollow space where his passion had once burned so bright.

Aaron's fingers twitched on top of the Walkman, beating out ghost rhythms. In his head, he still heard it - the beat that once lit him up. The music that made him, loved him, and broke him.

He thought of Eddie, lost to the seductive pull of chemicals and bass. Of Rachel, her smile forever out of reach. Of Havok, who had used him and discarded him like a broken record.

And always, always, the memory of that final night. The screams. The chaos. The devastating power of the "Death Tune" they'd unleashed upon the world.

A single tear ran down Aaron's weathered cheek. He closed his eyes, trying to shut out the memories, the regrets, the constant, gnawing emptiness.

"Look UP."

Nexus' words echoed in his mind, a ghostly whisper from the past. Aaron's eyes opened, startled by the vivid memory.

"Look up, man. It's all about the crowd. That's the real art of DJing. Reading the room, giving the people what they need before they even know they want it."

Aaron's gaze, so long fixed on the ground or lost in the middle distance, slowly began to lift. His eyes traveled up the weathered facade of the Masonic Temple, past the boarded-up windows and faded brickwork, to the night sky above.

Stars twinkled in the velvet darkness, a cosmic dance that had been playing out for eons, unnoticed by the lost soul on the steps below. Aaron's breath caught in his throat as he took in the vastness above him.

All those years searching for the perfect beat, digging deeper and deeper into the underground scene, and the answer had been above him all along. The rhythm of the universe, the music of the spheres - it had always been there, waiting for him to simply look up and listen.

The realization hit him like a physical force. The "Sounds of Hell" they'd unleashed... it had come from below, from the depths of human darkness and desperation. But the true music, the harmony that could heal rather than destroy, came from above.

At that moment, Aaron understood the true nature of music's connection to the spiritual realm. It wasn't just about rhythm and melody - it was about intention, about the energy poured into every note. The "Death Tune" had tapped into something primal and destructive, a force that fed on fear and chaos. But there was another kind of music, one that could elevate the soul and bring light to the darkest corners of existence.

Aaron's fingers, for the first time in years, fell still. The restless tapping ceased as he absorbed the celestial symphony playing out overhead. In that moment of quiet, he became aware of another sound - the soft strains of a hymn drifting from the church across the street.

"Amazing grace, how sweet the sound..."

The words floated on the night air, intertwining with the cosmic melody Aaron had only just begun to hear. He stood slowly, his joints protesting the movement, but his spirit lighter than it had been in years.

He looked down at the Walkman in his hand, the device that had been both his shield and his prison for so long. He removed the headphones, letting them dangle at his side.

The world rushed in - the rustle of leaves in the breeze, the distant hum of traffic, the laughter of late-night revelers. And beneath it all, the steady, comforting rhythm of his own heartbeat.

Aaron closed his eyes, swaying slightly as he let the sounds wash over him. For the first time in years, he felt the stirring of something long dormant within his soul - not the frenetic energy of his rave days, but something deeper, more profound.

He opened his eyes, looking once more at the church across the street. The hymn swelled, carried on the evening breeze. Aaron stepped forward, then paused.

Instead of heading towards the church doors, he turned his gaze upward once more. The stars twinkled at him, eternal and unchanging. A faint smile tugged at the corners of his mouth.

"I hear you," he whispered, to the stars, to the universe, to whatever higher power might be listening. "I'm ready to listen now."

Aaron pocketed the Walkman into his tattered fanny pack, but didn't move towards the church. Instead, he began to walk down the street, his steps slow but purposeful. His eyes remained lifted, taking in the night sky, the tops of buildings, the world above that he'd ignored for so long.

As he walked, the restless tapping of his fingers began again, but this time it was different. Instead of the frantic, desperate rhythm of before, it was steady, calm - the beat of a man finding his way back to the music of life itself.

Aaron didn't know where this new path would lead him. But for the first time in years, he felt a glimmer of hope. He had spent so long looking down, digging into the depths of his pain and regret. Now, finally, he was looking up - and the view was infinite.

The legend of the Sacajawea Junior High boys locker room and the "Sounds of Hell" would live on in Spokane's collective memory, whispered about in late-night diners and passed down to wide-eyed freshmen. But for Aaron, it was becoming just that - a legend, a cautionary tale from a past life.

In the silence between heartbeats, Aaron discovered the rhythm he'd been searching for all along - his own.

** **Footnote:** 0:21-1:29

...ring...ring...ring...ring...ring...

"Line one. You are on the air..."

Final page message encapsulation

message_final = "If you've made it this far, you can choose to go deeper. Ready for the next level?"

Activate hidden pathway

activate pathway ->

reveal link: https://bit.ly/3MiH8Kb

display: https://bit.ly/4dLAxnF

YOU'RE NOT ALONE

alternate_data = https://bit.ly/4fQVPBI

assist_link = https://chatgpt.the-supportive-specialist

 # Signal conclusion

signal_end transmission -> "All paths converge. [End of Storyline]"

If you or someone you know is struggling with mental health issues or experiencing suicidal thoughts, please seek help. There are resources that can provide support and assistance.

Helplines:

- **National Suicide Prevention Lifeline (USA):** 1-800-273-TALK (8255)
- **Crisis Text Line (USA):** Text HOME to 741741
- **Samaritans (UK):** 116 123
- **Lifeline (Australia):** 13 11 14
- **Canada Suicide Prevention Service:** 1-833-456-4566 or text 45645

Websites:

- **National Suicide Prevention Lifeline**
https://suicidepreventionlifeline.org
- **Mental Health America**
https://www.mhanational.org
- **Samaritans (UK)**
https://www.samaritans.org/
- **Beyond Blue (Australia)**
https://www.beyondblue.org.au
- **Crisis Text Line**
https://www.crisistextline.org

Encore:

"Raincry (Spiritual Thirst)" by God Within, Scott Hardkiss [128 BPM]

About the Author

As a dynamic and versatile radio professional, Aaron Traylor brings over 20 years of experience to the airwaves. His #1 rated daily music program airs across multiple US markets, earning him numerous "Best Radio Personality" awards. Aaron's talents extend beyond broadcasting - he's a published author, national mixshow producer, and TED Talks speaker on social media trends.

From hosting top-rated shows to managing brand operations, Aaron's career spans roles at major media companies like Clear Channel and CBS News. He's also the CEO of Crate Hackers, developing innovative DJ software.

A touring DJ who's performed alongside T-Pain and Kelly Clarkson, Aaron's passion for music, technology, and connecting with audiences drives his mission to push boundaries in the ever-evolving media landscape.

Read more at www.cratehackers.com.